The don
if she had stepped over a boundary way too soon. It was intimate, and yet he was a perfect stranger.

She was sharing this big old house with a man she didn't know, and yet for some reason she didn't feel afraid. She *did* feel on edge, but that had more to do with her reaction to him: his touch, for instance. What was that all about? Why had her heart started to race like a greyhound when his fingers had pressed down over her wrist? His dark brown gaze had locked her just as firmly in place—those bottomless eyes that saw so much and gave away so little.

She made a show of preparing the coffee, when in reality she would normally have settled for a teaspoon of instant. But Italians loved their coffee, right? She breathed in the fragrant aroma as the percolator did its job, her mind wandering as she thought about how long the sexy sergeant would be in town. *In her house.*

Dear Reader,

For a long time before I sat down to write this story, I had a strong sense of my hero, Sergeant Marc Di Angelo, even his body language and the way he spoke. I think he must have been downloaded from somewhere out in the ether into my head!

My heroine, Gemma, was also someone who was very alive to me. But that is the point of the story, really. Gemma is full of life and is embracing it as best as she can while living in the Outback town of Jingilly Creek. Meanwhile, Marc's job as a city cop has made him hardened and cynical. Even more than that, he's carrying a huge load of guilt.

Meeting generous-hearted Gemma with her crowd of loyal supporters affects Marc deeply because he is forced to face the things in life he no longer feels he deserves. It takes a lot to get Marc to open up his heart, and Gemma is the perfect person to do it.

Happy reading!
Melanie Milburne

P.S. I would like to thank Sergeant Iain Shepherd yet again for being my research person. You're the best, Iain!

THE MAN WITH THE LOCKED AWAY HEART

Melanie Milburne

Harlequin®

TORONTO NEW YORK LONDON
AMSTERDAM PARIS SYDNEY HAMBURG
STOCKHOLM ATHENS TOKYO MILAN MADRID
PRAGUE WARSAW BUDAPEST AUCKLAND

ISBN-13: 978-0-373-06781-7

THE MAN WITH THE LOCKED AWAY HEART

First North American Publication 2011

This edition published by arrangement with Harlequin Books S.A.

For questions and comments about the quality of this book please contact us at Customer_eCare@Harlequin.ca.

www.eHarlequin.com

Printed in U.S.A.

THE MAN WITH THE LOCKED AWAY HEART

To my brother Edgar John Luke.
Ed, you have been an amazing brother and a
real believer in me right from the start.
This one is for you with much love. XXX

CHAPTER ONE

'THERE'S someone here to see you, Gemma,' Narelle, the receptionist at the clinic, informed her as she popped her head around the consulting-room door.

Gemma looked up from the patient notes she was filling in before she left for the day. 'Not another last-minute patient?' she asked, trying to ignore the sinking feeling in her stomach. She had been working twelve hours straight and could think of nothing better than driving back to Huntingdon Lodge to catch up on some much-needed sleep.

'No,' Narelle said, and cupping her hand around her mouth in a conspiratorial manner added in a stage whisper. 'It's a police sergeant.'

Gemma straightened her slumped shoulders like a puppet suddenly pulled up by strings. 'A sergeant?' she asked. 'Why? What's happened?'

Narelle's eyes danced. 'He's the new cop. You know, the one we've been waiting for to replace Jack Chugg? He's in the waiting room. I guess he just wants to make himself known to you. Do you want me to hang around while he's here?'

Gemma pushed out from the desk and got to her feet. 'No, you go on home, Narelle. Ruby and Ben will be missing you. You've already stayed way past your usual time. I didn't realise Nick Goglin's transfer to Brisbane would take so long.'

'You think he's going to make it?' Narelle asked with a concerned frown.

Gemma hiked her shoulders up and down. 'Who knows? With head injuries it's always hard to predict the outcome. The neuro team in Brisbane will let us know as soon as he is assessed. All we can do at this stage is hope and pray he comes out of the coma with all his faculties intact.'

'Yes, well, all of Jingilly Creek is behind him, and of course Meg and the kids,' Narelle said. Her hand dropped from where it was holding the door ajar. 'I'll send your visitor in on my way out. Have a good one, Gemma.'

'Thanks,' she said as she quickly straightened the files on her desk. 'You too.'

Gemma heard firm footsteps moving along the corridor and then there was a brief hard knock on the consulting-room door a moment or two later.

'Come in,' she said, fixing a pleasant but professional smile on her face.

As soon as the door opened she felt her eyes widen involuntarily and her smile falter. For some reason she had been expecting a slightly overweight, close-to-retirement-age cop, someone who would take up the remote Outback post until they finally hung up their badge for good. She had pictured in her mind's eye a mid-height man with a balding pate and a belly that overhung his belt, similar to the recently retired Jack Chugg. She hadn't for a moment conjured up a tall, broad-shouldered, slim-hipped, dark-haired, gorgeous-looking man in his early to mid-thirties with a body that looked as if it would look even better without the covering of the blue denim jeans and white casual shirt he was wearing.

'Dr Kendall?' He moved across the floor to her desk in a couple of strides—most people took at least three or four—and held out his hand. 'I am Sergeant Marc Di Angelo.'

Gemma put her hand in his and immediately felt as if he had zapped her with a Taser gun. Electric jolts travelled from her palm along the length of her arm. And even more shocking, disturbing and totally inexplicably, her heart gave a funny leap and skip and trip movement behind the wall of her chest. 'Um—hi,' she said, feeling her professional front peeling away like shedding skin as she met his dark-as-espresso, coffee-brown eyes.

'I'm sorry to disturb you at the end of the day,' he said. 'But I have not long arrived in town and thought I should drop by and introduce myself.'

'Um…would you like to sit down?' she asked, waving a hand towards one of the two chairs she had positioned beside her desk so as not to intimidate her patients. Now she wished she had the barrier of her desk between the sergeant's long legs and hers. It seemed far too intimate a distance when he sat down soon after she had taken her own chair. If he moved his legs even a fraction, they would touch hers. He had powerful-looking legs, long and strong with well-developed muscles. She tried not to look at his quadriceps as they bunched beneath the fabric of his jeans but her gaze felt drawn to them as if pulled by some invisible force. She quickly fixed her gaze on his and her heart did another funny little stop-start. His eyes were so dark she felt compelled to stare at him. They were so dark and secretive, mysterious, closed off, locked down, as if he had seen too much and was not prepared to let anyone else catch even a glimpse of what it had done to him. 'Welcome to Jingilly Creek,' she said, working extra-hard at keeping her professional poise on track. 'I hope you enjoy your time here.'

His gaze was unwavering on hers and his expression—like just about all of the cops snthe had met in the past on business—was completely and utterly unreadable. 'From what I have seen so far, it is certainly going to be a change from the city,' he said.

In spite of his casual attire, Gemma could see the slick city cut to his jeans and shirt and the totally urban look he had in terms of grooming. The thick dark locks of his wavy hair were controlled by some sort of hair product, and his lean, fashionably unshaven jaw hinted at the potent male hormones surging around his body. She wondered why he of all people had taken such a remote post. She wondered too if he had brought anyone with him, a wife or girlfriend perhaps. She sidestepped her thoughts, annoyed at herself for even thinking about it. His private life had nothing to do with her. 'Yes, well, it's generally pretty quiet out here,' she said. 'But we have our moments.'

'How long have you been in town, Dr Kendall?' he asked, leaning back in his chair slightly, as if settling in for the rest of the evening.

Gemma shifted in her seat, her eyes flicking to those impossibly long, strong legs before returning to his dark, inscrutable eyes. 'I've been here three years,' she said. 'I came up from Melbourne. I wanted to do my bit for the Outback. There's a shortage of doctors in regional areas. It's obviously much the same for your people. We've been waiting for a replacement for Sergeant Chugg for nearly six months.'

He gave a slow nod. 'And what keeps you here, Dr Kendall?' he asked. 'It seems to me to be a rough, lonely sort of place for a young single woman.'

Gemma frowned at him. 'How do you know I'm single?'

His eyes went to her tightly knotted hands in her lap before coming back to hers. Was that a hint of mockery she could see in his darker-than-dark gaze? 'You're not wearing a ring,' he said.

'So?' she said, shifting again in her chair but in an affronted, agitated manner this time. Did she look as desperate and dateless as she sometimes felt? It had taken her the best part of her first year out here to put her heartbreak behind her. She was over it now. Well and truly over it. Or was there something about her appearance that shrieked lonely single woman? She knew she wasn't wearing any make-up to speak of and her blond hair was in need of new highlights, not to mention her roots, and she didn't even want to think about how badly her eyebrows needed a pluck. She would have done it last night but she had fallen asleep in front of the television. 'I might choose not to wear jewellery when at work,' she said. 'A lot of doctors don't.'

An upward movement of his top lip suggested it was about as close to a smile as he was used to giving. 'Point taken,' he said.

The ensuing silence was intimidating but, then,

Gemma wondered if he had intended it to be. He was obviously assessing her, summing her up for his mental database. Most cops did it. They were trained to read people, to decode even the most subtle body language and subtext of speech. She suspected he was a master at it. She sat it out as determinedly as she could. She crossed her arms and her legs, a lightning strike of sensation rushing through her when her ankle accidentally brushed against one of his. She thought she saw a flash of primal male interest in his gaze but he just as quickly went back to deadpan.

'You currently live at a property called Huntingdon Lodge,' he said. 'Is that correct?'

'For someone who's only been in town a matter of minutes, you seem to have done your research, Sergeant Di Angelo,' Gemma said with an arch look.

He gave a lift of one shoulder, a careless, casual movement she knew instinctively was a guise. 'In a town this small I don't think it will take me long to get to know everything there is to know about everyone.'

He said it as if that was his goal and Gemma could well believe he would achieve it if he set his mind to it. There was a steely determination to his personality. She could see it in the chiselled strength of his jaw, the Roman nose and in the firm, intractable line of his unsmiling mouth. Here was a man used to getting his own way in every facet of his life, she thought. The hint of arrogance in his persona, the aloof, brooding set to his features and his unmistakable attractiveness was a powerful and deadly combination she would have to take care to guard against.

'I've lived there since I came up from Melbourne,' she

said. 'Gladys Rickards was a patient of mine. She ran the homestead as a boarding house and farm-stay property after her husband died. I ended up staying on with her rather than finding my own place. She was lonely and liked the company. We became very good friends. I guess that's really one of the reasons I've stayed on for as long as I have in Jingilly Creek. I didn't want to leave Gladys. She became rather dependent on me towards the end.'

His gaze was still locked on hers. 'Mrs Rickards died not long ago, correct?'

Gemma shifted a little in her chair, her hands untying and then reknotting in her lap. She felt uncomfortable that he knew all that about her already. What else did he know? 'Yes. It was very sad,' she said. 'She was one of the mainstays of this community, everyone loved her. She will be greatly missed.' She let out a sigh and added, 'It's been just over a month and I still can't quite believe she's no longer there when I go home.'

The same brow lifted up, slightly higher this time, interest and intrigue there in that single movement. 'What did she die of, exactly?' he asked.

Gemma felt another frown pull at her forehead. 'She was eighty-nine years old, Sergeant. She had a long history of kidney problems associated with her type-two diabetes. She went into renal failure and at her request died at home.'

Dark, bottomless eyes, steady, watchful, assessing. 'You were with her?' he asked.

The question seemed loaded with something she found disturbing. She felt her back come up at what he seemed to be implying. 'Sergeant Di Angelo, I have been with a number of patients when they die out here,' she said. 'Jingilly Creek is a long way from dialysis and transplant facilities, any facilities, in fact. Even if those were options Gladys could have had, she chose to die at home. She felt she had lived a long and productive life. She wanted no further intervention. I felt it was a privilege to have taken care of her. She had been extremely kind to me when I first arrived in town.'

'She must have thought very highly of you,' he said, still watching her with the gaze of a hawk. 'Huntingdon Lodge is now yours, is it not?'

Gemma sent her tongue out over her lips again. Who on earth had he been speaking to? Ray Grant, the only other cop in town, hadn't even mentioned the arrival of the new sergeant and she had been with him just an hour ago at Nick Goglin's place. The only thing he had mentioned, and that had been at least a couple of weeks ago, had been that he was still waiting to see if the guy in mind was going to take up the position so he could have some much-needed time off. 'Look, Sergeant Di Angelo, I am not sure what you are suggesting, but I had no idea Gladys had written her will that way. It came as a complete surprise to me. I had not expected her to do anything like that. It was certainly never something we discussed.'

'How did her family feel about her bequeathing everything to you?' he asked, still with that cop-like gaze fixed on hers.

'Gladys and her husband Jim lost their only son forty years ago,' she said, trying not to fidget under his unnerving scrutiny. 'There are nieces and nephews and second cousins and so on, but no one who visited or kept in touch regularly.'

'So you were the lucky one to inherit all of her considerable assets.' It was neither a statement nor a question but more leaning towards an accusation, Gemma thought.

'Huntingdon Lodge is like a lot of old properties around here—quite rundown,' she said. 'It needs much more money than it produces in order to keep things going.'

'What have you decided to do with it?' he asked. 'Keep it or sell it?'

'I—I haven't quite decided,' she answered, which wasn't exactly the truth. As much as Gemma loved Jingilly Creek and caring for the locals, Huntingdon Lodge, although beautiful and with masses of potential, really needed someone with a farming background to run it properly. But for the first time since her mother had died she had a place to call home. But selling up and leaving so soon after inheriting the property could easily be misinterpreted by the locals. She had decided to make the best of it until enough time passed to make other plans.

'No immediate plans to head back to the big smoke?' he asked.

Gemma pursed her lips before she responded. He was watching her with that steady cop-gaze, quietly reading her every word and movement to see if they were in sync. 'I am not sure what these questions have to do with your appointment here, Sergeant. I should warn you that if you subject every person you meet in Jingilly Creek to the same inquisition you have given me, you might find your stay here is not as pleasant or productive as you might have wished.'

He gave her his brief version of a smile but it didn't involve his eyes. 'I'll risk it,' he said as he rose to his feet. 'Thank you for your time.'

Gemma stood up but her legs didn't feel as steady as she would have liked. The consulting room seemed to have shrunk considerably as it accommodated the sergeant's tall, authoritative presence. She could even catch a hint of his lemony aftershave and late-in-the-day honest male sweat. It wasn't unpleasant, certainly not as unpleasant as that of some of her hard-working, hard-drinking, hard-smoking patients.

Marc Di Angelo smelt of a man in his prime: sexy, virile and dangerously potent. 'How long are you planning on staying at this post?' she asked out of a politeness she didn't really feel.

'I am not sure at this stage,' he answered. 'It depends.'

'So, you're like doing a locum or something?'

His eyes gave nothing away. 'Something like that.'

'Have you had a chance to meet the other officer?' she asked. 'I was out on a call with Ray Grant earlier but he should be back at the station by now. He didn't mention he was expecting you today.'

'I spoke to him by phone a short time ago to let him know I was here,' he said. 'I'll head back there now to introduce myself in person.' He reached into the breast pocket of his jacket and handed her a card. 'My contact details in case I'm not at the station any time.'

Gemma took the card, which was still warm from being so close to his body. She put it on her desk, and faced him again. 'Where are you staying while you're here?' she asked, not just out of forced or fabricated politeness this time. Accommodation was limited in Jingilly Creek and he didn't seem the type to rough it at the local pub.

'The department has booked me in at the hotel for the time being,' he said. 'I believe it's called The Drover's Retreat.'

'Yes, well, it was a long time since it was anything like a retreat,' she said with a wry expression. 'You'll get a bed, a shared bathroom and a cold beer and bangers and mash, but that's about it.'

'Do you have somewhere else you could recommend?' he asked.

Gemma hesitated. Sharing Huntingdon Lodge with Marc Di Angelo was not something she was going to put her hand up for even if she was keen to get some regular boarders in to meet the cost of the repairs Rob Foster was helping her with. 'Um...well, there's not much around here. You'd have to go to Minnigarra for a motel but that's over a hundred kilometres away.'

He looked at her for an infinitesimal pause. 'So you're not currently taking in lodgers?'

Gemma knew her face was pink but there was nothing she could do about it. 'Um…I'm in the middle of repairs and renovations at present…' It sounded like the fob-off it was and the look in his dark eyes confirmed he recognised it as such.

'I'll give the local place a go before I make other arrangements,' he said. 'Thank you again for your time.'

Gemma let out the breath she had been unconsciously holding once he left the clinic building. She had a feeling this was not going to be the last time she was going to be cross-examined by the determined and rather delicious-looking sergeant.

The drive out to Huntingdon Lodge, especially close to sundown, never failed to inspire Gemma. The sky was a brilliant backdrop of orange and yellow against the red dust of the open plains. It hadn't rained for months but the last showers had been enough to fill the tanks and rivers for the first time in a decade. The pastoral area surrounding Jingilly Creek was still struggling to get back on its feet after such a difficult time but the locals were hopeful of another solid rain before winter arrived.

The long driveway to the stately old Victorian-style mansion was lined by old poplar trees, whose just-starting-to-turn leaves rattled like bottle caps in the evening breeze. A flock of corellas and sulphur-crested cockatoos called shrilly from the red river gums down by the river running through the property. It was a picturesque setting and yet Gemma felt a rush of loneliness when her gaze went to the empty rocking chair on the veranda.

Flossie, Gladys's old Border collie, came limping down the steps to greet her. Gemma crouched down and hugged the old girl around the neck. 'Hiya, Floss,' she said. 'I miss her too.'

The dog gave her a melting look and followed her into the house. Gemma fed the dog, and then, after a quick refreshing shower, she poured herself a cool drink and went back out to sit on the veranda to enjoy the last of the sunset. A couple of kangaroos were grazing in the house paddock, increasingly brave now that Flossie's eyesight and sense of smell and speed were not what they had once been.

A thin curl of dust rose from the road in the distance but Gemma couldn't make out if it was a neighbour or a tourist. Jingilly Creek hadn't exactly been a tourist destination since a bypass to the town had been built in the eighties, but very occasionally a visitor would find their way to the isolated community if they headed inland off the main highway. Gladys would always give them a warm country welcome, fill them with a good hearty meal and offer them a bed for a night or two. Gemma had enjoyed watching her landlady entertain 'city folk', as Gladys had called them. Gemma had reminded her that she too was a city girl, but Gladys had always insisted there just had to be country blood in Gemma's veins because she fitted in so well in the community. Gemma suspected Gladys had known how much she longed to fit in anywhere after so many years of feeling adrift. The Jingilly Creek community had become like an extended family to her. She felt loved and appreciated and valued and yet just lately it wasn't quite enough.

Within minutes another curl of dust appeared but this time, instead of continuing down the road, the car creating the plume turned into Huntingdon Lodge. Gemma got off the wrought-iron seat—she couldn't quite bring herself to sit in Gladys's chair—and held onto the veranda post as the gunmetal-grey car rumbled over the cattle grid. It continued on up the serpentine drive until it finally came to a halt in front of the grand old house with a spray of gravel as the brakes were applied.

She felt her chest give a little flutter when the tall

figure unfolded himself from the car, and her hand around the post tightened. He had undone a couple more of the buttons on his shirt, revealing just enough of his tanned chest to make her breath hitch in her throat. She suddenly was aware of her femininity in a way she hadn't been in years. She couldn't think of a time when she had met a more attractive-looking man. She used to think her ex-fiancé had cornered the market in good looks but Marc Di Angelo took it to a whole new level. 'Good evening, Sergeant,' she said as he crunched across the gravel towards the veranda. 'Taking in the sights, are we?'

His dark gaze ran over her pink T-shirt with 'Princess lives here' written across her braless breasts before slowly coming back to her eyes.

Too slowly.

Deliberately slowly, Gemma thought. She felt something in the air between them, something heavy and pulsing. She didn't want to think about just what it was.

'This part of the Outback is certainly worth a second look,' he said with a ghost of a smile playing about his sensually contoured mouth.

Gemma wondered how many female mouths had enjoyed being kissed by those sinfully sculpted lips. Her eyes surreptitiously went to his left hand and saw it was ringless. She wasn't sure why her belly did a little flip turn. Maybe she had spent too much time in the bush alone. 'What can I do for you, Sergeant Di Angelo?' she asked in a deliberately cool tone.

By this time his right foot was on the bottom step of the veranda and his right hand was holding the railing.

Flossie lumbered over, with her tail going from side to side, and he bent down and gave her a gentle ruffle of her ears, and the dog—shame on her—sighed as if in ecstasy. Gemma could see the muscles and sinews of his tanned arms liberally dusted with dark masculine hair that went all the way to the backs of his long fingers. His olive skin, along with his name, hinted at his Italian heritage, so too did the way he accented certain words, which suggested he spoke Italian fluently, although from his perfect colloquial English he was most certainly Australian born.

'Apparently there's no room at the inn, so to speak,' he said.

She frowned. 'That's ridiculous. Ron always has rooms free. He's always complaining how he hasn't had full occupancy for years.'

'Not this time,' he said. 'He told me I should ask you for a bed as you now own a guest house.'

Gemma's heart flipped like a pancake. 'Um…I'm not quite set up for guests…' She faltered. She waved a hand vaguely towards the house behind her. 'I'm still stripping the paintwork and refurbishing the place. As you can see, it's very rundown.'

His gaze moved past hers to take in the house. 'It looks fine to me.' His eyes met hers again. 'I'm prepared to pay my way. I can even help you with some jobs about the place in my spare time. I'm good with my hands.'

I just bet you are, Gemma thought with another furtive glance at his broad spanned hands. 'Um…well, then, I guess you can stay.' Not that I have much choice, she thought. She decided she was going to give Ron Curtis a piece of her mind next time she called in at the pub, and a very big piece at that.

She let the post go and brushed her damp palms down the sides of her faded trackpants. 'It's probably not what you're used to. I mean, it's a basic bed and breakfast and I can do an evening meal when I'm not out on a call or out on the plane with the Flying Doctor service.'

'You sound like you work long hours, Dr Kendall,' he said.

'I do, but, then, that's the Outback for you,' she said. 'I'm the only doctor this side of Minnigarra and the one there is semi-retired. The nearest hospital is Roma. All the serious stuff gets sent to Brisbane.'

'Do you have anyone else staying with you at present?' he asked.

'Er—no,' she said, suddenly wishing she had a house full of guests to dilute his disturbingly masculine presence.

He stepped back down from the veranda. 'I'll get my things from the car,' he said.

Gemma pushed her hand through her still-damp hair. Good grief, why hadn't she blown it dry and done her eyebrows while she'd had the chance? Had she even put on deodorant? And when was the last time she had shaved her legs, for pity's sake? That was the trouble with being single for so long. You stopped making the effort because there was no one worth making the effort for.

She watched as Marc Di Angelo popped the boot of his car, his biceps bulging as he lifted out a gym bag, a smaller suitcase and a laptop. He hooked one of his fingers through the neck loop on a leather jacket and draped it over his shoulder as he came back to the steps leading to the house.

She stepped aside to make room for him as he came up the stairs of the veranda. 'Welcome to Huntingdon Lodge, Sergeant Di Angelo,' she said, hoping Gladys wasn't turning in her grave at the insincerity in her tone.

Marc Di Angelo's dark brown eyes glinted with something indefinable. 'Thank you, Dr Kendall. I am looking forward to seeing what fringe benefits the bush has to offer.'

CHAPTER TWO

GEMMA showed him into one of the guest rooms, the one that was the most presentable and coincidentally the one furthest away from her room. His little comment about fringe benefits had made her awareness of him heighten. She felt the magnetic pull of his presence, the allure of his aloof, unknowable personality—a heady mix for a girl who hadn't had a date in close to four years.

She pointed out the main bathroom further along the hall on the second storey. 'Although we had fairly decent rain a few months ago, it's best to keep showers short,' she said. 'You never know out here when the next rain is going to fall. The meteorologists don't always get it right.'

'I am well used to water restrictions,' he said. 'Although I've lived in Brisbane for the last couple of years, I originally came from Melbourne.'

'Oh, really?' she said. 'What part did you come from?'

'I grew up in the outer suburbs,' he said. 'My parents ran a restaurant in Dandenong.'

'Were you stationed in the suburbs?' she asked.

'No, I was based in the city,' he said. 'Homicide.'

There was something about the way he said that word

that made Gemma's skin prickle. 'So, what brought you up to Brisbane?' she asked.

'I wanted a change of scene. A new challenge. A new climate.'

'Yes, well, Brisbane and Queensland in general will certainly give you that, compared to Melbourne,' she said.

'Do you miss your family, living so far away?' he asked.

Gemma thought of her father with his new wife and young family. He had remarried within four months of her mother's death in an accident. She still hadn't quite forgiven him for it. Her comfortable childhood home had been completely renovated and extended into an unrecognisable showpiece that had been featured in several home magazines. It was as if her stepmother had wanted every trace of Gemma's mother eradicated. Gemma's childhood bedroom had been knocked down to make room for a third bathroom no one ever used. 'No, not really,' she said. 'We pretty much live our own lives. If you'll excuse me, I'll make a start on dinner while you settle in. There are fresh towels in the bathroom if you'd like to freshen up before we eat.'

Gemma darted back to her bedroom and changed into jeans and a cotton shirt, this time with a push-up bra underneath. She ran a brush through her hair before pulling it back into a ponytail rather than leaving it hanging limply around her shoulders. She put on some deodorant and some perfume. She plucked out a few strays from her eyebrows and then gave her lips a quick swipe with some lip gloss. She could hear the shower going in the guest bathroom and tried not to imagine Marc Di Angelo standing naked under the spray of water.

She gave herself a vigorous mental shake. He might be gorgeous-looking but he was a cop. Most cops had control and power issues as far as she was concerned. Sure, they did a good job and there was certainly honour in protecting others at the risk of your own life, but she was not going to even think about getting involved in any way with a guy from the force. Besides, he was there as a professional and so was she. How would she appear to the locals if she launched into a red-hot affair with the first man who came striding into town? Desperate and dateless, that's how. She was already tired of the broad hints about her approaching thirtieth birthday and her single status. It seemed every patient thought it their mission to get her hitched before she hit the big three-oh. So far the candidates presented to her had done nothing for her. But Sergeant Marc Di Angelo was something else again, even if he was too attractive, too arrogant and too controlling for her liking.

She was in the kitchen, watching over the chicken pilaf she was cooking, when Marc Di Angelo came in. He had changed out of his shirt and was now wearing his blue denim jeans with a black T-shirt that clung to his perfectly formed biceps and pectoral muscles like a second skin. His abdomen was so flat she instantly sucked in hers. 'Dinner's not quite ready,' she said. 'Would you like a drink? I have wine, beer or soft drink and fruit juice.'

'What are you having?' he asked.

She gave the pilaf a good grind of black pepper. 'I

had a mineral water just before you arrived,' she said. 'I was thinking about having a glass of wine.'

'Are you on call?'

Gemma met his gaze as she put the pepper grinder down on the bench. 'I am always on call. That's the way it is out here. I am the only doctor in a radius of about two hundred kilometres.'

'Must be tough, not being able to let your hair down occasionally,' he said.

She shifted her gaze from the piercing intensity of his. 'I'm not much of a party girl in any case,' she said. 'I've seen the damage binge drinking does to young people. Lives can be changed in an instant and they can't always be changed back.'

'We see a lot of that in the city,' he said. 'I'm not a big drinker but I will join in you a single glass of wine.'

She chanced another glance at him. 'So you're not currently on duty, Sergeant?'

He gave her a quick movement of his lips that again was not quite a smile. 'Not at the moment. I came a week early just to get a feel for the place.'

'First time in the bush?' she asked.

His dark eyes glinted. 'Does it show?'

'A bit,' she said. 'But, then, I can't talk. It took me weeks to get used to everything. Time is slower out here. No one rushes unless they have to. It was frustrating at first but after a while you get used to it. Would you prefer red or white wine?'

'Red if you have it, but white is fine if not.'

'I'll…er…get some from the cellar,' she said, putting her wooden spoon down with a little thud.

'You have a cellar?'

'It's not mine—I mean, I didn't have it put in or anything,' Gemma explained. 'It's been here since the house was first built. In a climate as hot as this, it's too warm upstairs to keep good wines.'

'Mind if I come with you?' he asked.

Gemma would have refused his offer, except she absolutely loathed going down to the cellar. Gladys had always gone down there in the past, and then, when she had not been well enough to do so, Rob Foster, the handyman-cum-gardener, had always brought wine up for Gemma on the rare occasions she'd wanted it. The dark dank atmosphere of the cellar made her flesh crawl. It hadn't helped that on the first and only occasion she had gone down there alone a mouse had scuttled across the earthen floor right in front of her feet.

'Sure, why not?' she said, carefully disguising her relief. 'I might need your help in any case to lift up the trapdoor. It's over here at the back of the kitchen.'

Sergeant Di Angelo took over the opening of the trapdoor, lifting it as if it was a sheet of cardboard instead of solid timber with iron hinges. Gemma found the light switch and then she hesitated.

'Is something wrong?' he asked after a moment.

'Um—no,' she said, taking a deep breath and fixing her gaze on the sandstone steps.

'I'm happy to go first,' he offered. 'There might be spiders down there.'

Gemma felt her pride take a dive. 'Actually, that would be great,' she said with a tremulous smile. 'I'm not all that fond of spiders.'

She stood at the top of the steps as he went down and then once he'd given the all-clear she followed, but she stayed on the last step. 'I think the red stuff is over here,' she said, pointing vaguely to the left-hand side of the cellar.

Marc Di Angelo looked at her. 'Are you claustrophobic?'

Gemma rubbed her upper arms with her crossed-over hands. 'A bit, I guess.'

'You go back up,' he said. 'I'll get the bottle of wine. Is there any one in particular I should or shouldn't take?'

'No, just whatever,' she said, scooting back up the steps and hovering at the top. 'I don't think there's any Grange Hermitage or Hill of Grace down there.'

'You never know,' he said dryly, and bent at the waist to check out the labels as he pulled out various bottles.

Gemma couldn't stop looking at the way his jeans hugged his taut behind, or the way the muscles of his arms were so well formed. She was used to seeing well-used muscles out here in the Outback. The men were all toned from hard work on the land, but something about Marc Di Angelo's body made her feminine senses switch into overload. He was so damned attractive. Those eyes of his, so dark, like rich chocolate, and those lips of his, so sensual, and that strong, uncompromising jaw that gave him that don't-mess-with-me air.

Her insides did a funny little dance as he came back up the steps, carrying a bottle of wine. 'Here you go,' he said, handing her the bottle. 'I'll put the trapdoor back down.'

She watched as he closed the trapdoor, again lifting it as if it was a diet wafer before shooting home the bolt.

'So,' she said with an overly bright smile as she clutched the wine against her middle, 'no spiders?'

'None that I could see,' he said, dusting his hands off on his thighs.

She bit her lip. 'Um—you've got dust on your forehead.'

He wiped the back of his hand across his forehead. 'Gone?'

She shook her head. 'No, it's still there.' She balanced the wine with one hand as she pointed with the other to just above his left eyebrow. 'There.'

He gave his face another wipe but he somehow still missed the mark. 'All gone?'

Gemma felt his eyes lock on hers. The space between them was suddenly no space at all. He was standing so close she could see the darker circle of his black pupils in those incredibly brown eyes. She could even see the pinpoints of stubble on his jaw, the way it outlined every masculine contour of his face—his forceful chin, his firm upper lip, his fuller lower lip and the slopes and indentation of his lean cheeks. She could smell his cleanly showered smell. She could smell man and citrus rolled into one, fresh and sharp and dangerously tempting. Her breath hitched to a halt in her chest. Her mouth went dry. Her heart started to hammer and her legs felt strangely unsupportive.

'Here,' he said, and handed her a clean and folded handkerchief from his pocket. 'You do it.'

Gemma swallowed as her fingers curled around the fabric. Still clutching the wine to her chest, she lifted her other hand and wiped at the smear of dust on his forehead. Touching him, even through fabric, was like touching a live wire. She felt the kickback right up her arm. He must have felt something too for she saw his nostrils flare like those of a stallion and her heart gave another little stumble. 'I—I think that's it,' she said, in a voice that sounded like she was about fifteen years old.

'Thanks,' he said, stuffing the handkerchief into his back pocket.

Why doesn't he move? Gemma thought. She had nowhere to go; she was practically up against the wall in any case.

'Is there anything I can do to help with dinner?' he asked.

She suddenly remembered the simmering pilaf she had left unattended. 'Oh, my gosh,' she said, and thrust the wine at him. 'You open this while I check on the chicken. There's a corkscrew in the second drawer.'

'This one's a screw top,' Marc said.

'Oh, right.' She gave him a flustered sort of look as she lifted the lid on the dish she was making.

The smell of chicken and rice and Moroccan spices filled the air and Marc felt his stomach rumble in anticipation. The salad sandwich and instant coffee he had picked up at a roadhouse three hundred kilometres out of Jingilly Creek seemed like a long time ago.

But then his whole life seemed a long time ago.

That's how he saw things now: before and after. He was stuck in the after and there was no way he could replay his decisions and stay in the before, even though everything in him wished he could. A stint in the country was supposed to reset his focus. Get him back on track. Make him feel the buzz he'd once felt when going to work.

Make him forget.

The trouble was he didn't want to forget. The continuing nightmares about Simon bleeding to death in front of him were his punishment and he took it like a man. Simon's wife Julie's devastated face was another main feature during his dark, sleepless nights. And then there was his godson Sam, little innocent Sam who still didn't quite grasp that his father was never coming home. Marc dreaded the day when Sam would find out what had happened the day his father had died. How would the boy look on him then?

Forgetting was not his goal and neither was forgiving himself. That just wasn't going to happen in this lifetime. But distracting himself was something he needed to do. And this place looked about as far away as any place could be from his previous life as a city cop.

As soon as he had driven into this Outback town he had felt as if he had been in a time warp. The place looked like something out of an old movie, with its general store with its tall jars of old-fashioned sweets in the windows and its faded ice-cream cone advertisements on the walls outside. The one and only service station had a similar appearance, although its worn sign was well out of date with its petrol prices. He knew exactly why there had been a sudden shortage of rooms. Places as small as this soon got talking. A hot-shot sergeant from the city was not a welcome guest in a local watering-hole—bad for business. Everyone would think they would be nabbed for drink-driving or causing a disturbance or affray. No wonder Ron Curtis had sent him straight out to Gemma Kendall.

Not that she was all that welcoming either. She had grudgingly let him stay but it was pretty clear she was uneasy about it. Her recent inheritance had had his alarm bells ringing as soon as he had heard about it via the woman at the general store when he'd enquired about local accommodation options. It all seemed above board. No one in town suspected anything untoward, but Marc hadn't been a cop for thirteen years without having seen just about everything there was to see in terms of human greed.

Gemma Kendall was a cute little blonde who had supposedly come out here to do her bit for the bush, but she had just collected a windfall that by anyone's standards was a little unusual. Sure, this place was as she had said, a little rundown, but with a coat or two of paint and a few quick repairs it would fetch a fine price on the currently overblown property market. How had she done it? How had she got an old lady to rewrite her will in the last days of her life, leaving everything to her? Gemma Kendall was one smart cookie, that was for sure. Her innocent façade was convincing, a little too convincing, he thought as he watched her stir her delicious-smelling dish.

'So, what do you do out here in your spare time?' he asked after he had poured them both a glass of rich red wine.

She took a tentative sip before answering. 'I haven't had much spare time until recently,' she said. 'I'm usually pretty busy with the clinic and station visits, but then Gladys needed me almost full time by the end.

Narelle—that's the community nurse-cum receptionist you met this afternoon at the clinic—helped when she could. She's a widow with two kids. Her husband died four years ago. She juggles their property and her part-time work with me. Her mother helps but it's not easy for her.'

Marc took a small sip of the wine, which was surprisingly good. 'What happened to her husband?'

'Car accident,' she said, adjusting the heat setting on the cooker. 'He rolled his ute out on a back road. There was no doctor here at that point. He might have lived if there had been.'

'I suppose that's the problem with outlying areas,' he said. 'Time and distance are always against you.'

'Yes, that's true,' she said as she set out two plates and cutlery on the large kitchen table. 'We had another accident earlier today. A local farmer, Nick Goglin, came off his all-terrain bike. He's in a coma with head and probable spinal injuries. His wife and kids will be devastated if he doesn't make it. There's no way Meg will be able to run that cattle property on her own.'

'It's certainly a tough life out here,' Marc said, 'which makes me wonder why you've stuck it out for so long.'

Her grey-blue eyes met his across the table. 'Three years isn't all that long, Sergeant.'

He gave an assenting gesture with his mouth. 'Maybe not.' He picked up his fork once she had done the same. 'This smells great. Do you enjoy cooking?'

'Very much,' she said. 'What about you? Did your parents insist you work in the family's restaurant from a young age?'

Marc picked up his wine and gave it a swirl in the

glass. 'I spent a lot of time learning the ropes. There was certainly some expectation I would take on the business but my heart wasn't in it. My younger sister and her husband run the restaurant now.'

'Your parents are retired?' she asked.

'Yes, they travel a lot now,' he said. 'I have another sister who lives in Sicily. She's married with a couple of kids. My parents love spending time over there with them.'

She leaned her elbows on the table as she cradled her wine in both hands. 'So, what about you, Sergeant?' she asked. 'Is there a Mrs Di Angelo or Mrs Di Angelo-to-be back in Brisbane, waiting for you to come home?'

Marc held her gaze for a fraction longer than necessary. 'No rings.' He held up his left hand. 'No wife, no fiancée, no current girlfriend.'

Her grey-blue eyes rounded slightly. 'You are either very hard to please or hell to be around.'

His mouth twisted wryly because both were true to some degree. Even his sisters had told him bluntly he wasn't a nice person to be around any more. As to dating…well, he could certainly do with the sex, but he could no longer handle the expectation of commitment that so often went with it. He was a drifter, not a stayer. If you stayed too long, you got emotionally involved and that was the last thing he wanted. Not professionally and certainly not personally. 'What about you?' he asked. 'Is there a man in your life at present?'

She put her wineglass down, a delicate shade of pink tingeing her cheeks. 'Not currently,' she said.

'Too hard to please or too hard to be around?' he asked, his eyes gleaming.

'Too far away,' she said with a rueful expression. 'This place doesn't offer the greatest dating opportunities. The men out here tend to marry young, while most women my age have three or four kids by now. I'm not interested in being involved with someone just for the sake of it. Anyone can do that. I want more for my life. I want to feel connected intellectually as well as physically and emotionally.'

Marc leant back in his chair. 'So you're a romantic, Dr Kendall?'

Her eyes challenged his. 'Is that a crime?' she asked.

He leaned forward and picked up his wineglass again, frowning as he looked at the red liquid. 'No, of course not,' he said. 'It's just that sort of package doesn't come around all that often.' He sat back and met her eyes. 'You might be waiting for a long time for someone to come along who ticks all those boxes for you.'

'Better to have five years with the right one than twenty-five with the wrong one,' she said.

Marc felt a hammer blow of guilt hit him in the chest. Simon and Julie had been married five years. He had been their best man. He remembered the day so clearly. He had forgotten the rings and had had to get a colleague to bring them to the church in a squad car. Everyone had laughed, thinking it had been a set-up. So many memories. So many images of happy times he had shared with them both. Marc still remembered the day Simon told him he was going to be a father. He had been so proud and excited about building a family with Julie. There had been photos of Sam and Julie plastered all over Simon's desk at the station. Their anniversary had been the week before Simon had been killed. Marc had taken all of that away from them: their future; their hopes and dreams; their happiness.

The silence was measured by the sound of the large wall clock ticking near the pantry.

'What about you, Sergeant?' Gemma asked. 'Do you want to settle down one day?'

His eyes met hers but this time it looked like a light had gone off inside, leaving them like an empty, dark room. 'I am Australian born but, as you have probably guessed, I have a strong Italian background. Family is supposed to be important to us Italians, but I must be an aberration as I don't see myself settling down.'

Gemma pursed her lips. 'So you're a bit of a playboy, then, are you?'

He gave her that sexy not-quite-a-smile again, the glinting light back on in his eyes. 'I always make an effort to leave no casualties in the love stakes.'

'Have you ever been in love?' Oh, God, why did I just ask that? Gemma thought with a cringe of embarrassment. She took a quick sip of wine so she could bury her head in the glass.

'No, not unless you count the time I fell for my kindergarten teacher, Miss Moffat,' he said. 'I didn't miss a single day of my first year at school. My mother was very disappointed it didn't last. I had to be bribed to go most days, right up until I left high school.'

'School is often an issue for boys,' Gemma said. 'A lot of the boys out here drop out. It's sad to see the waste of potential.'

'What sort of social problems do you have out here?' Marc asked.

Gemma toyed with the last of her food, pushing it

around with her fork as she thought of the heartbreaking situations she had handled in the short time she had been in town. 'The usual stuff,' she said, 'drinking and violence and vandalism. It's a real problem with the indigenous youth. They're caught between two worlds. They don't really fit in either one at times. Some make it, like Ray Grant, for instance, but others don't. But it's much the same for the whites. The youth around here are bored as there is simply nothing for them to do if they don't work on the land. I try not to be overwhelmed by it but sometimes it's hard not to get involved. Clinical distance works a lot better in the city when you don't see past the name on the patient information sheet. Out here you know the patient personally and their parents, and the brothers and sisters. They're not just patients. Most of them become your friends.'

'You sound like you really care about your patients.'

'I do,' she said. 'Being a doctor in a small community is a huge responsibility. People depend on you in so many ways. But that's what I like about the job. You get to make a difference now and again. It's very rewarding when that happens.'

Gemma realised she had poured her heart out much more than she would normally do to a person she had only met just hours ago. It made her feel a little uncomfortable. He had much more information on her than she had on him. 'What do you love most about being a cop?' she asked.

'The long hours, the crappy pay, the criminals and the cold coffee,' he said.

She gave him a droll look. 'Very funny.'

His mouth tilted slightly. 'Did I mention the endless paperwork?'

'You didn't need to,' she said. 'It's the same in my profession.'

He put his knife and fork together on the plate in the correct I-am-finished position. 'Serving the public in law enforcement is always a challenge,' he said, his gaze momentarily focused on the wine in his glass. The light went off again. A shadow drifted over his expression, like a cloud over the face of the moon, but then he blinked and the shadow disappeared as he picked up his glass to add, 'You can't fix everything that needs to be fixed. You can't solve every case that needs to be solved.'

Gemma fiddled with the stem of her wineglass. 'So why Jingilly Creek?' she asked. 'Why not some resort town on the coast or somewhere more densely populated?'

His chocolate-brown eyes met hers, but apart from a tiny tensing movement in his jaw his expression remained unreadable. 'I felt like I needed a complete change,' he said. 'It seemed as good a place as any.'

'Did you throw a dart at a map?' she asked.

That brought a flicker of a smile to his mouth, softening his features for a moment. 'Just about.'

Gemma wondered if there was much more to his move out here than he was letting on. He had an air of mystery about him; an aloofness she suspected went much further than him simply being a cop. 'So you'll be the one in charge now at the station?' she asked.

'Yes,' he said. 'Constable Grant can now resume his regular duties.'

Gemma wondered how the new broom was going to fit in the broom cupboard down at the small station. In remote areas more junior officers often had to take on more senior positions due to the chronic shortage of staff. There would most certainly be an adjustment period. Jack Chugg had been strict but fair with the locals before he'd retired. Ray Grant had a much more laid-back approach, especially when dealing with other local indigenous people with whom he had blood ties. It would be interesting to see if Marc Di Angelo adopted the same live-and-let-live approach that Ray did. 'You might have to feel your way a bit,' she said. 'Ray's been used to handling things his way.'

'I'm here to do a job,' Marc said. 'Not win a popularity contest.'

Gemma studied his expression for a moment. 'It would be nice to do both, though, don't you think?'

He gave her a cynical look as he leaned back in his chair. 'Maybe I should take some lessons from you, Dr Kendall, on how to charm the locals,' he said. 'Who knows what bonuses might be out here for me to collect?'

Gemma set her mouth and began to rise to gather up their plates. Marc's hand came down over her wrist and held it to the table. The smile fell away from her mouth, her heart picking up its pace until she could hear it instead of the ticking clock. She felt the slow burn of his touch in his long strong fingers, so dark and masculine against the soft creamy texture of her skin.

'No,' he said. 'Let me clear away. You cooked. It's only fair that I get to do the dishes.'

She slipped her hand out from under his, her face

so hot she felt like she had stuck it in the oven on full fan-forced heat. 'Th-thanks,' she said. 'I'll make some coffee. I don't have any dessert. I mean, nothing I've made especially. I have fruit and yogurt, if you'd like?'

'Coffee is fine,' he said.

Gemma let out the breath she was holding as she opened the fridge to get out the ground coffee. The kitchen suddenly seemed far too small with Marc Di Angelo standing at the sink with his wrists submerged in hot, soapy water.

The domestic scene made her feel as if she had stepped over a boundary way too soon. It was intimate and yet he was a perfect stranger. She was sharing this big old house with a man she didn't know and yet for some reason she didn't feel frightened, or at least not in a physically threatened sense. She did feel on edge but that had more to do with her reaction to him: his touch, for instance. What was that all about? Why had her heart started to race like a greyhound when his fingers had pressed down over her wrist? His dark brown gaze had locked her just as firmly in place, those bottomless eyes that saw so much and gave away so little.

She made a business of preparing the coffee when in reality she would normally had settled for a teaspoon of instant. But Italians loved their coffee, right? She breathed in the fragrant aroma as the percolator did its job, her mind wandering as she thought about how long the sexy sergeant would be in town.

In her house.

Sharing the kitchen, the living spaces, the cutlery and crockery, his lips resting on the rim of the same cup she might have used the day before, his lips closing over a fork she had put in her mouth previously. It had never felt like this when Gladys had had guests staying before. The middle-aged couple from Toowoomba, for instance. They had stayed for two weeks and not once had Gemma thought about the towels that had wrapped around their bodies in the bathroom, or the water that had cascaded over them in the shower, or the sheets that had covered them while they'd slept.

The mere thought of Marc Di Angelo in the shower had sent her pulses soaring and this was only the first day. What would it be like in the morning? Would she hear him shaving, or perhaps singing or humming to himself, or was he one of those grumpy types who didn't properly wake up until ten in the morning or until a double shot of caffeine hit his system?

'Where do you want these put?' Marc asked, jolting her out of her reverie.

'Oh…' Gemma said, flustered again and unable to disguise it in time. 'Um…the cutlery goes in that top drawer over there and those plates in the cupboard above.'

She watched as he reached up and stacked the plates, his arms so tanned, so strong, so arrantly male. She swallowed when he turned his head and locked gazes with her. 'Is something wrong?' he asked with a quizzical look.

She shook her head, running her tongue out over her lips. 'Um, no, not at all,' she said. 'I was just thinking how I have to stand on tiptoe to get into that cupboard.'

His hand closed the cupboard while his gaze

remained centred on hers. 'You seem a little uptight, Dr Kendall.'

'That's ridiculous,' she said, folding her arms across her middle but just as quickly unfolding them as she realised how her body language was contradicting her denial. 'Why would I be uptight? This is a guest house. You are a guest.'

'Maybe you should call me Marc as we're going to be living together,' he said.

Gemma felt her cheeks heat up again. Did he have to make it sound so intimate? Had he done that deliberately, knowing it would unsettle her? It worried her that he was seeing so much more than she wanted him to see. Those eyes of his were so penetrating and dark, his expression so level and composed, while she was sure she was giving off all sorts of clues to her discomfiture. 'Marc, then,' she said, forcing a stiff smile to her lips.

'Am I your first house guest since you inherited the property?' he asked leaning his hip against the counter.

Gemma reached for the coffee cups, embarrassed at how she betrayed herself yet again by allowing them to rattle against each other as she put them on the bench. 'Yes, the first since Gladys died, that is. We had a run of guests a few weeks before she went downhill. The rains we had in the spring brought a few extra tourists our way to see the wildflowers.'

'Do you mind if I call you Gemma?'

Hearing her name on his lips sent a shower of sparks down her spine. It was like a rolling runaway firecracker bumping against each and every vertebra. 'Um…of course not,' she said. 'No one stands on ceremony in

Jingilly Creek.' She picked up the tray she had put the coffee and cups on. 'Would you like to have this outside on the veranda? It's probably nice and cool out there now, or at least cooler than inside.'

'Sure, sounds good,' he said, and took the tray from her.

Gemma stepped back, her fingers burning where his had brushed against hers in the handover. She told herself to get a grip, but it didn't really work. Her eyes kept going to the taut shape of his buttocks as if drawn by a magnet as he walked out to the veranda.

He set the tray down on the table between the two wrought-iron chairs, politely waiting until she sat down before he did so. The sound of Flossie's toenails clip-clipping along the floorboards as she came out to join them was the only sound in the still night air.

The night sky was dark as ink, thousands of stars peeping through the velvet-blanket canopy. An owl hooted from one of the sheds and a vixen gave her distinct bark in the distance as she signalled for a mate. Flossie pricked up her ears but then gave a long drawn-out too-tired-for-all-that-now sigh, and rested her greying head back down on her paws.

Gemma shifted forward on her chair. 'How do you have your coffee?' she asked.

'Just black, thanks.'

She poured it for him and handed it over with a wry smile. 'Sorry I haven't got any doughnuts.'

The light coming from inside the house was soft but it was enough to see the glint of amusement reflected in his gaze. 'Not all cops live on coffee and doughnuts,' he said.

She sat back in her chair, carefully balancing her coffee cup in her hands. 'It's a tough job,' she said after taking a sip. 'It must be awfully stressful and heart wrenching at times.'

He paused before he spoke, and again she saw that fleeting shadow pass across his gaze before it shifted from hers. 'Yes, it is but no one forced me to do it. I chose it. And I will stick with it unless it becomes obvious there is nothing left for me to achieve.'

Gemma gave her coffee an unnecessary stir. His statement seemed to be underlined with implacability. There was a steely determination in his character she found both attractive and a little unnerving. She couldn't think of a single person she had met before who was quite so determined, quite so focused and quite so disturbingly, dangerously attractive. She could imagine him working on a case, uncovering information that others would surely miss. His sharp intellect and his ability to read people and situations would make him a formidable opponent for any criminal deluded enough to think they could outsmart him.

The owl hooted again, the swish of its wings as it flew past the veranda on its way to the shearing shed sounding exaggerated in the stillness of the night.

'This seems a rather quiet appointment for someone who has worked in a busy city homicide department,' Gemma said. 'We haven't had any murders out here for decades.'

He took another leisurely sip of his coffee before he spoke. 'I am sure I'll find plenty to do to pass the time.'

The sound of the phone ringing indoors brought

Gemma to her feet. 'Excuse me,' she said. 'I'd better get that. I'm waiting for news of Nick Goglin's progress.'

Marc put his cup down, stood up and walked to the edge of the veranda. Leaning on the railing, he looked up at the twinkling stars of the Milky Way. At the funeral he had heard one of Simon's relatives tell his little boy Sam that his daddy would always be watching out for him up there in the night sky, no matter where he went. 'Which one are you, mate?' Marc asked, but of course there was no answer.

CHAPTER THREE

'GEMMA.' One of the volunteer ambulance officers, Malcolm Gard, was on the other end of the line. 'We've just got news of a roll-over out on the Bracken Hill Road. A passing motorist called it in. We're on our way now but it might be best if you meet us out there. It sounds bad.'

'I'm on my way,' she said, and hung up the phone.

Marc came in from the veranda with his mobile phone up to his ear. 'Right, I'll go with Dr Kendall,' he said, and hung up.

Gemma snatched up her doctor's bag and mobile phone, which she had been recharging on the kitchen bench. 'Was that Ray?' she asked.

'Yes, he'll meet us out there,' he said. 'Would you like me to drive?'

'No, I'd better drive. I know the road better than you do,' she said. 'Flossie, come in, girl.'

The dog obediently came in and settled on the doggy bed near the back door, next to her bowl of water.

Gemma didn't like admitting it but it was rather reassuring having someone with her on the journey out to Bracken Hill Road. The road was unsealed and interspersed with potholes and, of course, out here there were no streetlights. Although the night was clear, the bush seemed dark and threatening as it loomed either side of the winding road. The thought of breaking down out here, even with a mobile phone with her for back-up, was a little frightening. She didn't feel quite so unsafe with Marc Di Angelo on board, although he threatened her in other ways. She was acutely conscious of him sitting in the passenger seat, his long legs taking up far more space than any other passenger she had carried before. He'd had to put the seat back to its furthest position as soon as he'd got into the car. She could smell his aftershave now he was a little closer to her than when they had been sitting on the veranda. The lemon-based scent teased her nostrils, making her think of how the rest of his body would smell even closer up.

'You drive well, considering,' Marc said.

'Considering what?' Gemma asked, instantly bristling. 'That I'm a woman?'

'No,' he said. 'Considering this road is rough and there are kangaroos and wombats, possums, dingoes and foxes in that bush.'

'I know they are there,' she said. 'I've seen three kangaroos so far.'

'Only three?' he said. 'I counted four.'

Gemma didn't chance a glance at him as that particular stretch of road took every bit of concentration she possessed. As she rounded the next bend she could see the lights of a car turned upside down against a tree about half a kilometre ahead. Another car was pulled over to the other side of the road. The driver, she assumed, was the person who had reported the accident.

'How far away is the ambulance?' Marc asked, checking over his shoulder.

Gemma glanced in the rear-view mirror and breathed out a sigh of relief when she saw the glow of lights coming around one of the bends in the distance. 'Not far now,' she said. 'Malcolm's not the fastest driver out here. He's one of the older volunteers. He doesn't take too many risks.'

The person who had called for help was a local, Bill Vernon. He was visibly shaken by coming across the accident and rushed over as soon as Gemma and Marc got out of the car. 'I found her like that,' he said, pointing to a girl lying on the gravel roadside. 'I reckon she's hit a roo and rolled the car. She can't have been wearing a seat belt.'

'Thanks for staying with her, Bill,' Gemma said, as she set to work assessing the patient. 'Do you know who it is?'

'Nuh, never seen her before,' he said. 'She's only young.'

She was at that, Gemma found out as she examined the girl. Aged about nineteen or twenty, she was unresponsive so Gemma put on a hard collar, privately relieved that Bill Vernon hadn't moved the girl in case she had neck or spinal fractures. The ambulance had arrived so within a few minutes Gemma had oxygen running and with assistance from Marc and Malcolm and the other volunteer, Dave, who was even older than Malcolm, they got the girl on to a spinal board, and Gemma established IV access.

While the ambulance drove back to town, Gemma rode in the back and worked on resuscitating the patient with Dave's help. Ray Grant had turned up just as they had been leaving the accident site. He stayed behind to conduct the accident investigation with two officers on their way from Minnigarra, who Marc had called as back-up. Marc had offered to drive Gemma's car back to the clinic and was leading the way.

The patient didn't respond to voice stimulus and Gemma could see she had right facial abrasions and a scalp haematoma. There was blood at the girl's mouth and her breaths were shallow and short at fifty per minute.

Gemma got Dave to take the girl's pulse and BP and put on the pulse oximeter and ECG dots while she redid the primary survey. The patient was clearly developing an obstructed airway so Gemma got Malcolm to stop the ambulance, and with Dave stabilising the patient's neck she loosened the cervical collar and intubated the patient. There was no ventilator in the ambulance, so Gemma had Dave hand-ventilate the patient while she pushed the IV fluids.

Once the patient was transferred into the clinic treatment room, with Marc assisting the older men, Gemma was better able to assess the level of injury. There had been a progressive drop in blood pressure after the patient had been hand-ventilated, but there was no apparent blood loss to account for it. She cut off the patient's T-shirt and bra to reveal an extensive left chest abrasion and haematoma. There was bony and subcutaneous crepitus, indicating a flail segment. When she listened to the chest with a stethoscope, there was no air entry on the left, which had become hyper-resonant to percussion, the trachea was deviated to the right and the neck veins distended, indicating she had developed a left tension pneumothorax. Gemma had deliberately done EMST, or ATLS as it was better known abroad, before she'd come out into the country—unrecognised and untreated tension pneumothorax was one of the killers in the 'golden hour' after severe trauma.

Gemma inserted a large-bore cannula into the front of the left chest and air hissed out, with rapid improvement in blood pressure and ease of ventilation.

She got Dave to assist her as she inserted a left chest drain to complete the immediate management of the chest injury, talking him through it as she knew he wasn't all that confident. It was at times like these that she thought of the well-equipped and super-trained paramedics she had met while working at a large city teaching hospital in Melbourne. They were so adept at handling just about any situation that by the time the patient got to the resus bay at the hospital they were stabilised and ready for definitive care.

Out here, with just volunteers and minimum equipment, Gemma sometimes felt as if she was all alone in the Outback. Patients lived or died according to her expertise and calm in the face of panic-ridden situations, even though at times she herself felt very much like panicking. This was nothing like playing doctors and nurses with friends in the back garden when she had been a kid. This was about real people's lives and real futures in her hands. People who had loved ones, families who would be torn asunder by the loss of their son or daughter, husband or father, wife or mother. Gemma had felt it herself when her mother had been struck by a car while crossing the road. One minute your loved one was alive and breathing and the next they were dead. Gone for ever.

She caught Marc's dark eyes as she reached for more IV fluid to run in saline at full bore, and got ready to insert a second IV cannula. 'You were a great help out there,' she said. 'You've obviously worked in Traffic at some stage.'

'Yes,' he said. 'Seen a lot of things I wish I hadn't seen.'

'Yeah, I know that feeling,' she said as she glanced over at Dave. 'Pulse and BP, Dave?'

'Pulse one-thirty and BP ninety over sixty,' Dave informed her.

The patient began to respond to painful stimuli and Gemma's further examination revealed tenderness over the left upper abdomen.

'What do you think?' Marc asked.

'It's hard to say with any certainty but I think she might have a ruptured spleen,' Gemma answered. 'But we don't have any imaging facilities here.'

'So what happens now?' he asked.

'I'll do a secondary survey to exclude other major injuries,' Gemma said as she prepared to insert a nasogastric tube and urinary catheter. 'And then she will have to go to Roma. They've got a general surgeon there, and ultrasound—if she's got a ruptured spleen she'll bleed out without a laparotomy before they get anywhere near Brisbane. When they've stopped the bleeding, she'll go to Brisbane for neurosurgical assessment.'

Gemma had relayed the clinical details to Arthur Rogers, the general surgeon in Roma. Once the patient was back in the hard collar and supported by sandbags and a spinal board, Gemma supervised the return to the ambulance. However, Malcolm was complaining of tiredness and Dave too was dropping not-too-subtle hints about the trip to Roma.

'How about I drive the ambulance while one of you guys rides in the back with Dr Kendall?' Marc said. 'Constable Grant is still at the accident site with the Minnigarra guys.'

'It's all right,' Gemma assured the ambulance volunteers. 'He's the new sergeant. He knows how to drive.'

'Yeah, we heard about him from Ron Curtis,' Malcolm said, exchanging a quick look with Dave.

Gemma was soon in the back of the ambulance with the patient and Dave as back-up. Via the ambulance radio, she relayed a clinical update to the hospital at Roma. She was also able to give the girl's name so the family could be contacted as Marc had found her purse in the overturned car and got the information from her licence as well as her mobile phone. Gemma had been impressed by his calm, manner of working in the background. He had helped where he could, but he had also switched into cop mode, making sure the road was clear of debris and that everyone had put on their fluoro vests in case of another car coming around the bend without warning. He had also delegated responsibilities to Ray without taking over completely. And he was driving the ambulance with the sort of competence that was sadly lacking in the regular volunteers. The trip would normally take a couple of hours but after a quick peek at the highway sign they had just passed, Gemma thought they might take thirty if not forty-five minutes off that.

* * *

Once the patient was handed over at Roma, Dave expressed a desire to spend the night at his daughter's house. She only lived a few streets away from the town centre. Gemma was pretty sure it wasn't because he felt uncomfortable around Marc. She thought it had more to do with some sort of matchmaking attempt. The looks Malcolm and Dave had exchanged back at the clinic seemed to suggest something was cooking. She gave Dave a questioning look but he pointedly avoided her gaze. It was only as he got into his daughter's car once she had pulled up in front of the hospital that his expression became sheepish.

Marc turned to her with a twitch of his lips. 'Was it something I said?'

Gemma gave her eyes a little roll. 'I think it has more to do with me, actually.'

'Oh?'

'Yes,' she said, deciding it was better to have it all out in the open. 'Ever since I've been in Jingilly Creek the locals have taken it on themselves to try and find me a husband. It's apparently absolutely appalling to them that I am twenty-nine years old and still unattached.'

'So I am to be the current candidate, is that it?' he asked with an amused look as he opened the ambulance door for her.

Gemma's gaze moved away from his as she got into the vehicle. She waited until he was back behind the wheel before she said, 'Look, if you just ignore it, they will soon get the message. It's embarrassing, I know, but they mean well.'

'I'm not the least bit embarrassed,' he said, pulling away from the hospital.

She swung her gaze to him. 'You're not?'

He gave a one-shoulder shrug. 'You're a dedicated doctor, a very skilled one, I might add— I've seen a few bumbling their way through accident scenes. And you can cook. Oh, and you're not all that bad in the looks department.'

Gemma arched her brows at him. 'Not all that bad? What is that supposed to mean?'

He gave her another twitch of his lips that was all she was going to get in terms of a smile. 'I think you know what I mean, Dr Kendall.'

Gemma sat back in the seat and mused over his comment. At the time her ex-fiancé's betrayal had hit her hard. And although she liked to think she had mostly put it behind her, the knockout punch to her confidence had left its mark. She still found it hard to find anything but fault with her looks. Like a lot of women, she had issues with her body. She would have liked to have been taller than five-six and she would have liked fuller breasts and a flatter stomach, but generally she was content to have a healthy body, which was more than a lot of people had, even at her age or younger. She had never forgotten a young patient of sixteen during her training who had been diagnosed with osteosarcoma. A keen athlete with her whole life ahead of her, Madison McDougal had died after extensive treatment, including the amputation of her leg. It had made Gemma thankful for her own health and strength, and whenever she felt herself preparing for a pity-party over her broken dreams she recalled that young girl's courage to regain perspective. She wasn't sure what to make of 'not all that bad in the looks department' but it was certainly gratifying to know Sergeant Di Angelo had taken a second look.

The trip back to Jingilly Creek was over before Gemma realised it. She felt the ambulance come to a halt outside the clinic and jolted upright. She blinked her sleepy eyes and sent Marc a rueful look. 'Sorry, I must have fallen asleep.'

'Just as well you weren't driving,' he said with a wry expression.

They drove back to Huntingdon Lodge in Gemma's car, and again she let him take control. She was much more tired than she had realised after treating the accident victim. The level of concentration and sense of responsibility had zapped her energy, especially on the back of Nick Goglin's accident earlier in the day.

It was now well after midnight and Flossie barely lifted her head off her paws when Gemma and Marc came in.

'Would you like a hot or cold drink or something?' Gemma asked, pushing back her hair, which had worked loose from her ponytail.

'No, I'm cool,' he said. 'You look exhausted. Is this a usual day for you out here?'

'No, thank God,' she said, reaching for a glass to have a drink of water. 'Mostly it's pretty quiet. The clinic days can be hectic, of course, but it's not usually as crazy as today has been.'

'What time do you head into town in the morning?' he asked.

'I have a clinic that starts at eight-thirty,' Gemma said. 'I have a couple of house calls in the afternoon—elderly patients who can't always make the trip to town.'

She put her glass down on the draining-board. 'Please help yourself to cereal and toast and whatever in the morning if I'm not here. Everything is in the pantry over there or in the fridge. I'm sorry I can't offer the sort of service Gladys was renowned for. She would have cooked you a full breakfast.'

'You don't have to wait on me,' he said. 'I am quite capable of looking after myself.'

'Right, then,' she said, tucking another loose strand behind her ear. 'Well, goodnight. Oh, and thanks for your help tonight. It was much appreciated.'

'Glad to be of service,' he said.

There was a beat or two of absolute silence. Even the clock on the wall seemed to have stopped, as if the second hand had frozen.

Gemma dropped her gaze from the dark intensity of his and slipped out of the kitchen, her heart beating a little too fast and too jerkily as she made her way upstairs to her room.

The moon was behind a cloud when Gemma woke from a deep sleep. She usually had no trouble getting to sleep—it was staying asleep that was the issue. It had been worse since Gladys had died. The big old house seemed so empty, and the various creaks and groans of the timber floorboards or staircase had made her wish more than once or twice she had more than an elderly deaf and almost blind dog for company.

She lay on her side and looked out of the window, waiting for the cloud to pass over the face of the moon, her thoughts drifting to a few doors down the hall where Sergeant Marc Di Angelo was sleeping. She had given him the king-sized bedroom, figuring with his tall body he would need the extra length. She couldn't stop herself imagining him there, perhaps lying on his stomach, the sheets draped over his taut buttocks, or maybe he was a back sleeper, his arms flung out wide, his muscular chest rising and falling as he slept. She wondered if he slept naked. Her mind conjured up his tanned toned body in all its glory. She had seen her fair share of male bodies, in all shapes and sizes, but she had a feeling Sergeant Marc Di Angelo's body would be cut and carved to perfection.

She rolled on her back, taking one of her pillows with her and hugging it to her chest. She blew out a sigh of frustration. Why couldn't she just switch off her brain and go to sleep? It was always worse after a late-night emergency. She would ruminate over the whole scene, checking and double-checking she had performed the correct procedure or followed the right protocol. She thought of that girl's parents, how they would feel to be informed their daughter had been badly injured in a car crash. She could just imagine the worry they would feel, she had seen it so many times in ICU back in Melbourne: the haunted, haggard faces of loved ones who could only hope and pray for their child or relative to pull through.

Gemma turned back to look at the moon, which had now peeped out from behind the cloud. She closed her eyes and began to relax each of her muscles in turn as she had learnt years ago in a yoga class. Her toes, her ankles, her shins, her knees, her thighs—

She sat bolt upright in bed, her eyes wide open, her heart beating like frantic wings inside her chest. She listened as ice-cold fear dripped drop by drop down the entire length of her spine.

There was a faint scratching sound behind the wainscoting of her room. And then she heard a tiny squeak and then another.

She flung off the bedclothes and bolted out of the room, calling out for Flossie as she went. 'Flossie? Floss? Come here, girl.'

'Is something wrong?' Marc appeared from his room, a towel draped around his hips, one hand holding it in place.

Gemma pulled up short, her heart still drumming a tattoo behind her ribcage, but now it went up another notch. 'Th-there's a m-mouse in my room,' she stammered. 'Actually, I think there's probably hundreds in there, maybe even a plague of them. I heard them behind the wall. I have to get Flossie.'

Marc frowned as he tightened the towel about his hips. 'I'm not sure poor old Flossie is going to be much help. Do you want me to have a look?'

'Oh, would you?' Gemma asked with wide, grateful eyes.

'Have you had a problem with mice before?' he asked as he led the way back to her room.

Gemma kept well back in case any of the little pesky rodents took it on themselves to head out into the hall. 'Gladys always dealt with it in the past,' she said, hovering in the doorway. 'But mostly when we had them they were downstairs in the kitchen or the laundry, but then Rob filled in the holes where they were getting through.'

'Rob?' Marc asked as he bent down to press his ear against the bedroom wall. 'Who is Rob?'

'Rob Foster. He's the local handyman,' she said. 'He's been doing work out here for Gladys for years.' She watched with bated breath as Marc listened intently. After a long pause she whispered, 'Can you hear anything?'

He let out a breath and rose to his full height. 'Not a thing,' he said. 'Do you think you might have been imagining it?'

Gemma felt her face heating because of what she had been imagining before she'd heard the squeaks. 'Of course I didn't imagine it,' she said with an affronted toss of her head.

'Maybe you should sleep in another room,' he suggested.

'Yes.' She rubbed her upper arms as if it was twenty below zero. 'I think I'll do that.'

His eyes meshed with hers, a stretch of silence pulsing like electricity along an invisible wire that seemed to be connecting her to him, pulling her inexorably closer and closer.

Gemma felt her belly turn over itself, a flicker of feminine awareness travelling downwards all the way to the apex of her thighs. In case he could see what effect he was having on her, she quickly lowered her eyes from the searing intensity of his to stare at the muscular perfection of his naked chest. He had a masculine covering of hair that went from a fan over his broad chest before it narrowed down his abdomen, ridged with muscle, disappearing below the towel he had slung around his lean hips. Her eyes widened a fraction and her throat threatened to close over. There was a hint of arousal behind the fabric of the towel and the tension in the air suddenly skyrocketed.

She slowly brought her gaze back up to his, something in his eyes reminding her that she was standing before him in a satin tank top and shorts pyjama set that was outlining every single contour of her body. 'Um…I'm sorry for disturbing you in the middle of the night,' she said, stepping away from the door to stand out in the hall.

He followed her, closing the door of her room behind him.

She licked her lips and rambled on, 'I suppose you think it's terribly cowardly of me to be so scared of a tiny mouse but I just can't help it. I can't stand them.'

His expression was back to deadpan. 'Maybe you need to think about getting yourself a cat.'

'Yes,' she said, biting at her lip. 'I guess I should.'

'I can set a trap for you if you'd like.'

'I can get Rob to do it,' Gemma said. 'You're not here for pest control.'

'Not those sorts of pests perhaps,' he said dryly.

She gave him a tight smile. 'Well, goodnight, then,' she said, stepping back and cannoning into the antique washstand. 'Ouch!'

Marc stepped towards her, his hand coming down over her arm, his long fingers wrapping around her wrist. 'Are you all right?' he asked. 'You hit that pretty hard.'

Gemma felt clumsy rather than bruised, although her rear end had taken rather a knock. But it was her face rather than her bottom that felt like fire, and her wrist where his fingers were holding her burned like it had been branded with his touch. 'I—I'm fine,' she said.

His eyes locked with hers in another moment of silence. She saw the flare of his pupils, she felt the subtle tightening of his hold, as if he sensed she was about to pull away. Her breathing rate escalated, her heart rate creeping up as the silence stretched and stretched and stretched.

She wondered if he was thinking about kissing her.

She was definitely thinking about kissing him.

She could just imagine how that firm mouth would feel pressed against hers.

Was he thinking about kissing her? It certainly looked like it. His dark chocolate eyes had flicked down to her mouth, lingering there for an infinitesimal pause. She saw the slight movement of his jaw as if he was preparing his mouth for the descent to hers. Her belly imploded with the thought of his tongue slipping between her lips, thrusting into her mouth to tease and tangle with hers.

'You really should watch where you are going,' Marc said, suddenly releasing her wrist. 'If something happens to you, what will happen to the community of Jingilly Creek? It could be weeks if not months before they find another doctor to replace you.'

Gemma blinked herself back into the moment. 'A bruised behind is not going to kill me. I've suffered much worse.' Like the bludgeoning of my ego, she thought. Why hadn't he kissed her? Had he downgraded her from 'not bad in the looks department' to 'quick, cover all the mirrors in case she cracks them'? She decided she had been in the bush for too long and for too long alone. She was fantasising about a man she had only just met. What on earth was wrong with her? Even when she'd lived in the city she had never been one to develop silly crushes or infatuations. Her one serious relationship had developed slowly over time. She had enjoyed having someone to go out with, although at times she had found the intimate side of things a bit of a chore. She hadn't felt much passion with Stuart, but she had always blamed it on the long hours she'd worked. It had been a vanilla relationship, as one of her friends had called it after the break-up in an effort to cheer her up, after finding Stuart was to become a parent with one of the oncology nurses.

Gemma couldn't imagine anything vanilla about Marc Di Angelo. Everything about him suggested there would be blistering passion and heat and fire in his arms. All she had felt so far had been his fingers—twice now—and her flesh was still tingling. When she looked into his eyes, as she was doing now, she felt as if he was heating her up from the inside out. She felt tremors of desire deep and low in her body, ripples of want that refused to go away. Her breasts felt sensitive under the satin covering of her shortie pyjamas, her nipples tight and erect. Her tongue slipped out to deposit a film of moisture over her lips and she held her breath as his black-ink eyes followed the movement.

'Things could get very complicated around here if I do what I think you want me to do right now,' he said in a deep, rough-sounding tone as his eyes locked back on hers.

Gemma put up her chin haughtily even though she knew her hot face gave her away. 'What makes you think I want you to kiss me?'

'You know you don't have to pretend there's a mouse in your room to get a man to sleep with you,' he said. 'There are other ways to get his attention.'

Her mouth dropped open as wide as her eyes and it took her a moment to get her voice to work. 'You think I would sleep with you when I've only just met you?'

His brushed the broad pad of his thumb across the fullness of her bottom lip, a little half-smile playing about his mouth. 'I'm damn sure you would. At the very least you'd like to kiss me right now.'

Gemma rubbed at her buzzing lip as if he had burnt it, which it felt like he had, but that was beside the point. 'Your confidence is misplaced, Sergeant Di Angelo,' she said in a prim manner. 'I have no intention of kissing you, either now or some time, any time, in the future.'

'Fine. You're not going to kiss me, I'm not going to kiss you.' He stood looking down at her for another pulsing beat of silence. 'Do you want to put money on that?' he said with a glint in those black-as-pitch eyes.

She put her hands on her hips, her chin still high. 'How much?'

'How much are you prepared to lose?' he asked.

Gemma was incensed at his arrogance, incensed and a little bit excited too, which was really rather disturbing when she came to think about it. 'I'm not going to lose, Sergeant Di Angelo,' she said with some misplaced arrogance of her own.

'We'll see about that,' he said, and before she could spin on her heel and make her outraged-female-stalking-off-with-her-chin-in-the-air exit, he had gone back to his room and closed the door.

CHAPTER FOUR

WHEN Gemma came down to the kitchen in the morning she saw through the window, as she filled the kettle, Marc's tall figure running up the driveway. He was dressed in T-shirt, shorts and trainers, each of his long strides kicking up a little puff of dust as he went. He looked magnificently fit. Lean and strong, and although as he drew closer to the house she could see he had worked up a sweat, he looked nothing like she would have done if she had tried to cover even a quarter of the distance he had run.

She drew in her stomach and sighed. She couldn't even remember the last time she had gone for a jog. It was usually too hot for her to do much more than walk, and because Flossie always wanted to come too, it wasn't exactly a pace that got her heart anywhere near the training zone. She decided it was time to get back into the pool, or at least in the river in the case of Jingilly Creek. Before Gladys had become so unwell Gemma had swum almost daily at a watering-hole she had found along the river running through Huntingdon. It was like an oasis in the middle of the bush, lush and green, the pendulous branches of the willow trees that fringed the curve of the river offering both privacy and shade. There wasn't time for her to swim now but she made a promise to herself to get back to it this afternoon once she got home.

Marc came in the back door, bringing with him the smell of the bush and vigorous exercise. He stopped to ruffle Flossie's ears before straightening to look at Gemma. 'Off to work?' he asked.

'Yes,' she said. 'I've left a key for you on the bench so you can come and go as you please. Flossie has a pet door but she only uses it if no one is here to let her in and out.'

'Fine. I'll be off once I've had a shower,' he said. 'I thought I would to go to Minnigarra to introduce myself to the officers there. I should be home about six.'

Home.

How domestic and intimate he made it sound, Gemma thought as she scooped up her keys and purse and sunglasses. 'Have a good day, Sergeant,' she said.

'Didn't we decide to drop the formalities, or are you worried it might blur the boundaries for you?' he asked.

She raised her chin. 'Have a good day, Marc,' she said with pointed emphasis.

'You too, Gemma,' he said with his first real smile. 'Don't work too hard.'

Gemma couldn't get his smile out of her head all the way to town. Or his eyes. Those dark-as-chocolate eyes that seemed to see through her clothes no matter what she was wearing. She had felt a little exposed last night dressed in shortie pyjamas, but this morning she had felt exactly the same dressed in a cotton shirt and trousers.

The first-name thing was dangerous, she thought. It added another layer of intimacy she wasn't sure was wise given they were already sharing a house. The bet they had agreed on worried her too. For some reason, possibly because it was forbidden now, she wanted nothing more than to feel his mouth on hers. She wanted to taste him, to taste the maleness of him, the potency and power she could sense he had in full measure. She found herself wondering who and what sort of women he had dated in the past. Work colleagues or women he had met casually? Was he a casual sex person or a serial monogamist? She didn't have to stretch her imagination too far to know he would be a monumentally satisfying lover. Not that she had a lot of experience compared to other women in her age group, but something about his aura of command and competence and confidence made her certain he would know his way around a woman's body like a maestro did a Stradivarius violin. She felt the pull on strings of desire deep and low in her body every time he looked at her. God only knew what would happen if he took her in his arms and followed through.

Narelle was at the clinic, setting up, when Gemma came in. She looked up from booting up the computer and grinned delightedly. 'So the sexy sergeant is staying out at your place, is he?'

Gemma narrowed her eyes resentfully. 'Only because Ron Curtis pretended he didn't have a room.' She dropped her purse and keys on the desk with a thud and a clatter. 'Can you believe that? He's got fifteen rooms.

He's always complaining no one uses them any more. I'm going over there as soon as I get a chance, to tell him what I think of him.'

Narelle swung back and forth on her ergonomic chair. 'You have to admit it's a whole lot nicer out at Huntingdon Lodge than at the pub.'

'That's beside the point,' Gemma said. 'If Gladys was still alive, it wouldn't be a problem.'

Narelle's tawny brown eyes twinkled mischievously. 'So you think you need a chaperone, do you? What, has he made a move on you already?'

Gemma felt her face flush and bent to put her keys and purse in the drawer under the desk to disguise it. 'Of course not,' she said crisply. 'He's not my type, in any case.'

'Come on, Gemma,' Narelle said. 'He's every woman's type. He's tall and gorgeous to look at and you only have to look into those sleep-with-me eyes to know he'd be fantastic in bed.'

Gemma schooled her features into indifference, even though those strings inside her body twanged yet again. 'I'm not interested. He's too arrogant for my liking.'

'It seems to be he's not so much arrogant as sure of what he wants and how to get it,' Narelle said, and she reached for the phone as it began to ring.

Which is exactly my point, Gemma thought as she went through to the consulting room.

Gemma worked her way steadily through her list of patients before she headed out of town to a property called Hindmarsh Downs, owned by the Hindmarsh family for six generations. Elizabeth Hindmarsh, the matriarch of the family, was in her early nineties and suffering from dementia. The family wasn't keen on sending her to a care facility several hundred kilometres away, but it was clear that looking after a frail and confused old lady was taking its toll, particularly on Janine Hindmarsh, Elizabeth's daughter-in-law.

'How is she today?' Gemma asked as Janine met her at the homestead door.

'Irascible as ever,' Janine said with a worn-out look. 'I found her out in the veggie patch stark naked except for her slippers this morning. Just as well none of the stockmen were around.'

Gemma held back her smile at the thought. 'It must be so trying for you, keeping an eye on her with all the rest of the stuff you have to do.'

'Tell me about it,' Janine said. 'Joe helps when he can but he feels uncomfortable dressing or helping his mother in the bathroom, so just about everything falls to me.'

'Have you thought any more about a rest home for her?' Gemma asked.

Janine shook her head. 'Joe won't hear of it. His grandparents died on Hindmarsh property and so did his father. He wants Elizabeth to be buried in the family plot in Jingilly Creek too. I just have to cope.'

'Maybe we could see if there's someone in town who can come out and help you on a daily basis,' Gemma suggested. 'I can ask around or a put an ad up in the café or the pub. You never know, there might be someone who would be grateful for a few hours' work.'

'I guess that could work,' Janine said. 'Even if someone was to help me shower her a couple of times a week, or just sit with her and listen to her hark on about old times. She tells me the same story over and over again. It's so draining to have to pretend you are interested.'

'Yes, that is a pattern of age-related dementia,' Gemma said. 'Typically the past is recollected in accurate detail but when it comes to what she did yesterday or five minutes ago, she will be vague or not remember a thing.'

Janine led her through to the large family sitting room where Elizabeth was sitting staring out of the window, muttering to herself.

'Mother, the doctor is here to see you. Dr Gemma,' Janine said. 'Do you remember her from the other day? She had a listen to your heart and your breathing.'

Elizabeth turned her snow-white head and glared at Gemma before she addressed her daughter-in-law. 'I don't want to see any doctor. And I'm not going to answer any of those silly questions either. Fancy asking me what day it is or what the Prime Minister's name is. Does the silly little chit think I'm off my head?'

'Mrs Hindmarsh, I just want to check your blood pressure and listen to your chest this time,' Gemma said. 'Would that be OK?'

The old woman shifted in her chair like an old broody hen ruffling her feathers. 'I'm not sick,' she grumbled. 'I haven't been sick for a day in my life. I haven't spent a day in bed, not once, not even when I had the children. I was back in the kitchen, cooking the meals for the workers, you ask Henry. He'll tell you. Get him in here, Janine. Get Henry to tell this young lady I don't need any fancy pills or potions.'

'Mother, Henry's been gone for ten years,' Janine said rolling her eyes at Gemma.

'Gone?' Elizabeth frowned. 'Gone where? What are you talking about? Of course he's not gone. I was speaking to him just this morning about the cattle in the river paddock. They'll have to be shifted in case it rains.'

'It's not going to rain, Mother,' Janine said in a long-suffering tone. 'Now, just let the doctor listen to your chest.'

Gemma took out her stethoscope and warmed it in her hand for a moment before she raised the old woman's blouse to listen to her heart. There was a faint murmur and when she moved the stethoscope to Elizabeth's back to listen to her breathing she could hear the sound of fluid at the base of the lungs. She straightened and put the stethoscope back in her doctor's bag. 'I think we'll have to keep a close watch on your chest, Mrs Hindmarsh,' she said. 'There's a possibility you could develop pneumonia if that fluid builds up any more.'

'Phffft,' Elizabeth said with a scowl.

Gemma put the blood-pressure cuff around the old lady's bony arm and watched as the portable machine recorded the figures. 'Your blood pressure is a little bit higher than normal but nothing to be too worried about.'

Elizabeth tugged her arm away almost before the cuff was off. 'Told you I'm not sick.'

'I'll come and see you tomorrow, OK?' Gemma said.

'Do what you like,' Elizabeth said, still scowling. 'But don't expect me to count backwards from a hundred.'

Gemma said goodbye and followed Janine out to the kitchen.

'Would you like a cuppa?' Janine asked.

Gemma wanted to get going but she was sure Janine was desperate for company, or at least for company other than that of a demented and difficult old lady. 'Sure,' she said with a smile. 'That would be lovely.'

Janine filled the kettle at the sink and then carried it over to the bench to plug it in. 'I've heard the sergeant's quite good-looking,' she said as she reached for the teapot and cups. She turned around and smiled at Gemma. 'I also heard he's boarding out at Huntingdon Lodge.'

Gemma pursed her lips. 'Yes, well, it wasn't my idea.'

Janine put some home-made cookies on the table. 'But I thought you wanted to take in boarders? Wasn't that the plan to help with the upkeep of the place?'

'Well, yes, but I have a lot of work to do before it's ready for guests,' Gemma said.

'Isn't Rob helping you with that?'

'Yes, but he's not able to do the heavy stuff with his back being so touchy,' Gemma said. 'He promised to come around today and do some stripping back of the paintwork in the hall. That will be a big help.'

Janine smiled as she handed Gemma a cup and saucer. 'Maybe the handsome sergeant will help you. Joe said he's a strong, fit-looking man. How long's he staying with you? Do you think he will get his own place eventually?'

'I'm not sure,' Gemma said, pushing the image of Marc's strong, fit body out of her mind with limited success. 'I get the feeling this is an interim thing for him. I can't see him sticking it out here in the bush. He has city cop written all over him.'

Janine sat down and leaned her elbows on the table and rested her chin in her hands. 'You're what, nearly thirty, right?' she said. 'Don't you think it's time you went looking for a husband? Before you know it you'll be forty and it will be too late to have kids, or too late without help. You don't seem the single, career-driven type, Gemma.'

Gemma felt an all-too-familiar pang when she thought of the possibility of spending the rest of her life alone. It wasn't that she was still pining for Stuart. She had come to realise over her time out in the bush that their relationship would not have lasted the distance even without his infidelity. It was more about where she was in her life now. She wanted to settle down, to have a family with a man who loved her, a man who would be faithful and true to her. She knew that by staying out here in the bush she would be reducing her chances of meeting someone, yet she couldn't quite bring herself to leave. She felt at home here, and that sense of belonging was going to be hard to give up, and even harder to find in a big city if she did. 'It's not exactly raining men out here, Janine,' she said, picking up her cup and taking a sip of the hot, refreshing brew.

'That's true enough,' Janine said, handing over the cookies. 'Is the dashing sergeant single?'

Gemma took a cookie from the plate, renewing her vow to swim that afternoon. 'Apparently.'

Janine's brows waggled up and down playfully. 'You never know, Gemma, he might be the one for you.

Anyway, even if he's not the one, a little fling with him wouldn't hurt. God knows, you've had no social life out here. You've got to take what comes along when it comes along.'

'Would you be suggesting I have a fling with Marc Di Angelo if he was nudging retirement or twenty years older and divorced with adult children?' Gemma asked.

Janine chuckled as she topped up their teacups. 'He must be more gorgeous than Joe let on. Go for it, Gemma. He's hot, he's hetero and he's here. Make the most of it, my girl.'

Gemma drove back to town to pick up some supplies for dinner. She was across the road from the pub at the general store when she heard shouting. The doors of the pub burst open and two local men fell brawling into the street. They were followed by some of the other drinkers, including the owner/manager of The Drover's Retreat, Ron Curtis.

'Break it up, you two,' Ron said. 'I won't have no fighting in my pub, d'you hear?'

There were a couple of grunts from the two men while a few more punches were thrown. The dust was being stirred up so much it was hard to know who was getting the worst end of the deal. Gemma winced as yet another wildly flung punch was thrown. She could see where this was going to end. Her day would be made longer by having to stitch up someone's face or splint a couple of broken fingers. Alcohol was a real problem with some of the locals, particularly the younger ones. Although they were legally able to access alcohol, they had yet to learn there were limits. It frustrated Gemma to see them abuse their bodies in such a way for the long-term risks were well known now and the costs to the community high.

A tall figure suddenly appeared from around the corner and strode towards the scuffling men, grabbing both by the scruff of the neck in each of his hands. 'OK, guys, let's cool it,' Sergeant Marc Di Angelo said, 'otherwise someone might get hurt.'

One of the men spat at Marc and the other tried to take a swipe but Marc's hold was too firm and his arms too long for the guy to reach his face. 'You don't want to go down for assaulting a police officer, do you?' Marc asked.

The younger of the two men was a patient Gemma had seen a few weeks ago for stomach pain, which had turned out to be a nasty case of gastritis. She had warned him then of the dangers of heavy drinking but it seemed her warning had gone unheeded. Darren Slateford was heavily inebriated as his words were slurred when he spoke. 'S-sorry, m-mate,' he said, staggering a little as Marc released him. 'I didn't realise who you were.'

The other man was only slightly less under the weather. Gemma could now see through the covering of dust and blood that it was Trent Bates, who at the best of times was a bit of a troublemaker in town. But on this occasion he must have realised he was outmatched and held up his hands in a gesture of surrender. 'It's cool, it's over,' he said.

Marc let him go just as Gemma approached to see if she could help Darren, who had a nasty split in his lip, which was bleeding profusely.

It all happened so fast Gemma didn't quite understand why she was suddenly flat on her back on the ground with her head thrumming like a bell struck with an anvil.

A short, sharp swear word from Marc cut the air like a knife. He lunged for Trent and had him with his arms behind his back, issuing a warning of arrest just as Ray Grant came on the scene. Marc handed Trent over with a grim statement to charge him. And then he was on his knees in the dust, leaning over Gemma, concern etched on his face. 'Are you all right, Gemma?' he asked, brushing the hair back from her forehead.

'I…I think so…' She put up her hand and felt the stickiness of blood on her forehead. 'Ouch.'

'That jerk hit you instead of me,' Marc said. 'I should have seen it coming but I didn't realise you were so close. Are you sure you're OK? Not dizzy or seeing double?'

'Are my pupils even?' Gemma asked, wincing at the pain in her head.

He peered into her eyes. 'Yep, they're even, a bit large, though.'

'That's OK, then,' she said, trying to sit up.

'Here, let me help you,' he said, scooping her up out of the dirt as if she weighed next to nothing.

Gemma wasn't quite sure if she was seeing stars because she was being carried in Marc's strongly muscled arms or because she had taken a punch to the head. It felt amazing to be held against his fit, toned body. He was all hard muscle and she could smell his distinctive smell of lemon and the musk of afternoon sweat. Her breast was rubbing up against him with each stride he took, a delicious sensation that made her already spinning head spin some more.

Narelle was at the clinic when Marc carried Gemma through the door. 'Oh, my God, what happened?' she asked.

'A stray punch hit her in the head,' Marc said grimly.

'I'm fine, really I am,' Gemma said. 'Stop making such a fuss.'

'I'd better dress that for you,' Narelle said, inspecting the wound. 'It doesn't look like it needs stitching. A Steri-Strip ought to do the trick.'

'She's already bruising,' Marc put in as he laid her down on the examination table.

Gemma breathed in his breath as it skated over her face. It was minty and fresh with just a hint of coffee. 'I feel such a fool about this,' she said. 'I should have stayed well clear. I know what Trent's like. He's got authority issues.'

'Yeah, well, he's going to be seeing a little more of authority figures if I have my way,' Marc said as he stepped aside for Narelle to set to work. 'I'd better give Ray a hand back at the station. Will you be OK until I get back?'

'Of course I will. Ouch!' Gemma said as Narelle applied Betadine to the wound.

'Look after her,' Marc said to Narelle as he headed out.

'I will,' Narelle trilled, giving Gemma an up-and-down movement of her brows once he had left the clinic. 'My, my, my, I do believe you have a knight in shining armour at your beck and call.'

'Don't you start,' Gemma grumbled, wincing again as the Steri-Strip was eased in place.

'Seriously, Gemma,' Narelle said as she took off her gloves. 'When was the last time a handsome man swept you off your feet? He's absolutely gorgeous. I'm so-o-o jealous. I wish someone would come and carry me off into the sunset. Mind you, he'd have to be pretty strong since I'm carrying twenty pounds I shouldn't be carrying.'

'He carried me to the clinic,' Gemma said with a note of pragmatism. 'And it was my own stupid fault.'

'Are you sure you feel all right?' Narelle asked, gently feeling over the back of Gemma's skull for any signs of haematoma.

'I'm fine except for a bit of a headache,' Gemma said. 'I think I'll go home and lie down.'

'Ah-ah-ah.' Narelle shook her finger at her admonishingly. 'No driving for twenty-four hours after a head injury, remember?'

Gemma scowled as she swung her legs over the examination table. 'I can see I've trained you a little too well.'

'You have to be careful, Gemma,' Narelle said, her expression serious again. 'You've got a nasty bruise forming. I'll get an ice pack to put on while we wait for Sergeant Di Angelo to come back to take you home. I'll get one of the guys to drop your car around tonight.'

There was that word again: home, Gemma thought. Now the whole town would be talking about her and the sexy sergeant getting it on. It wasn't that it wasn't a tempting thought. It was, perhaps too much so. But her pride was on the line here. He was only in town temporarily. What would be the point in having a fling, as Janine had advised, when her heart could get broken when it ended, as it most surely would? She wanted much more than an affair. She longed for companionship and commitment, for loyalty and love. It was a tall order in today's climate of casual relationships but she couldn't help feeling the way she did. She wanted to be a mother. She wanted to have it all—the career and the children and the husband. A husband she could trust with her life and her love.

She gave a heavy sigh and laid her aching head back down on the pillow. Did such a man even exist these days?

CHAPTER FIVE

'How are you feeling?' Marc asked a little while later when he returned.

Gemma began to sit up and he supported her by the arm as she hopped down from the examination table. He was struck again at how petite she was compared to him. He towered over her, especially when she wasn't wearing shoes. He could smell her perfume. It had lingered on his clothes from when he had carried her across the street. Holding her so close had made him regret the bet he had made with her. He wasn't keen on losing anything in life, but a bet was a bet. It would be interesting to see who broke it first.

Her mouth fascinated him. It had a little upward curve of the top lip, like a bee sting. Her lower lip was full too, soft and pillowy and utterly kissable. He could just imagine what it would feel like under the pressure of his. He had spent most of the night before thinking about it, which certainly made a change from having vivid nightmares about Simon. Who would have thought someone as attractive as her would be out here in this wasteland of a town? An affair would pass the time certainly, but she looked like the type of girl who wanted to play for keeps. He had once been the sort of man who would have done so. He had wanted what Simon had had. He had been actively searching for it…

But that had been before.

'I'm fine except for a slight headache,' she said as she hunted for her shoes.

Marc found them and lined them up for her to slip her narrow feet with their pink-painted toenails into.

She looked up at him sheepishly. 'I hope you didn't arrest Trent. He didn't mean to hit me.'

'No, but he meant to hit me,' Marc said. 'That's an offence that will be dealt with by the court. I'm sending him to Roma with Constable Grant. He will be probably be fined and given a good-behaviour bond.'

'Was Ray OK with that?' she asked with a frown.

'Constable Grant is no longer in charge,' Marc said as he helped her get off the table. 'I am.'

She didn't answer but meekly took his arm as he led her out to his car. It was an intoxicating feeling, having her lean on him; it made him want to draw her closer, to pull her up against his body and feel her softer contours mould against his harder ones. She smelt divine, some sort of light, flowery, fresh fragrance that teased his nostrils. Even with her clothes dusty and with a colourful bruise on her forehead she looked gorgeous. She was exactly the girl-next-door type his mother had her heart set on him finding and keeping. He quickly pushed the thought aside. He wasn't playing for keeps. He couldn't play for keeps.

'Thanks for coming to my rescue like that,' she said as he helped her into the passenger seat. 'But I was concerned about Darren's lip. That's why I came over when I did. I could see he was bleeding badly. Narelle had to stitch it for him. He came into the clinic after you left.'

'You should know better than to approach a situation like that,' Marc said. His gut still churned when he thought about how a single punch could have killed her. He had seen too many tragic deaths caused by the effects of excessive alcohol. People often lost control and hit out, not stopping to think of the consequences. Sometimes they didn't even remember their actions the following day. The lives of both victims and their assailants were ruined. It was a lose-lose situation and it frustrated him that it seemed to be getting worse, not better.

'I know,' she said on an expelled breath.

He sent her a quick glance as he put the car into gear. 'As long as you're all right,' he said. 'That's quite some bruise you've got there. How's the one on your behind?'

Her cheeks took on a rosy hue and she turned to look out of the window. 'It's perfectly fine, thank you.'

Marc suppressed a smile as he drove out of town towards Huntingdon Lodge. He would have loved to check it out for himself but he wasn't going to make things any harder for himself than they already were.

Gemma woke after a long sleep. Marc had insisted she rest and she had obeyed, feeling relieved she could legitimately have a few hours off. She came downstairs to the smell of food, some sort of meat dish that was aromatic with Thai herbs and spices.

'I hope you're hungry,' Marc said as she came in. 'I

took the liberty of taking over the kitchen. I hope you don't mind.'

She perched on the nearest stool. 'Of course I don't mind. I just feel a bit embarrassed you've had to fend for yourself. Gladys would be turning in her grave.'

'I am sure she would think it perfectly acceptable for me to take care of you after such an incident,' he said. 'You could have been killed, you know.'

Gemma bit down on her lip. 'Yes, I know. I treated a patient in Melbourne who died after a pub brawl. He was only nineteen. It was such a tragic waste of a young life. The guy who hit him wasn't even a bad guy. He had never offended before. He'd just had too much to drink.'

'Not all victims end up in the morgue,' he said.

Gemma saw the shadow pass over his features again and the grim tightness about his mouth. What horrors had he seen in the course of his work? Was that why he was out here in the bush? Was he suffering from some form of post-traumatic stress disorder? Should she ask or just leave it to him to tell her in his own time? She had hated talking about her break-up in the early days. It had taken some months before she could speak without tearing up. But after a while she had moved on. Maybe Marc too just needed some time.

The meal was delicious and although Gemma had decided against drinking any wine, she still ended up feeling light-headed after sitting opposite Marc while they ate and chatted about inconsequential things. He offered to make coffee while she sat on the veranda to watch the moon come up over the horizon.

Gemma breathed in the cooler night air. The sound of

crickets and frogs around the tank stand reminded her of how far away she was from her previous life in the city. She loved it out here, but as she drew closer to her thirtieth birthday she couldn't deny feeling a little restless. Returning to Melbourne didn't really appeal—she felt as if she didn't fit in any more. Her father was busy with his second family and most of her friends had moved on with their lives, some of them busy juggling careers and children. Her time out in the bush had changed her. She had grown to appreciate the wide open spaces, the fresh air, the rhythm of the land, the turning of the seasons, the scorching heat and the precious rain, the dust and the flies, but most of all the friends she had made. She was needed out here, not just for her skills as a doctor but as a member of the community. But it worried her that by staying out here she might miss out on what she wanted most.

Marc came out with a tray bearing coffee. 'Is your head still hurting?'

Gemma straightened on her seat. 'No, not at all now.'

He put the tray on the table next to her. 'You were frowning.'

'I often frown when I'm thinking.'

'What were you thinking?' he asked as he poured the coffee.

'Nothing important.'

Marc sat on the other chair and picked up his coffee. 'I forgot to tell you I met your odd-job man, Rob Foster,' he said. 'He and another local guy came round while you were sleeping to drop off your car. He didn't stay long. He didn't want to disturb you while you were resting.

He put some poison down for your mouse and he set a couple of traps before he left.'

Gemma suppressed a little shiver. 'I always feel a little guilty about using poison and traps. It seems so cruel.'

'Life is cruel, Gemma,' he said as he took a sip of coffee.

She looked at him in the light of the moon. There was a frown pulling at his brow, and his jaw had tensed up again, as if he was clenching his teeth but trying his best to disguise it. 'Why did you take this post, Marc?' she asked.

His eyes were hard and impenetrable when they met hers. 'Why do you ask?'

'I could be wrong but I get the feeling you're not here because you really want to be.'

He raised one of his brows mockingly. 'So you fancy yourself as a bit of a detective, do you, Dr Kendall?' he asked. 'What else have you decided about me?'

'You're cynical and you automatically think everyone is a criminal.'

'I would be a fool to take everything and everyone at face value,' he said, 'even someone as convincing as you.'

Gemma stood up and went to the railing. She gripped it so tightly her fingers ached. She took a deep breath before turning back to face him. 'So you still think I somehow manipulated Gladys into changing her will, don't you? Do you trust anyone, Sergeant Di Angelo?'

His gaze remained steady on hers but his expression gave nothing away. 'There have been many cases recently of elderly people being exploited by their relatives,' he said. 'Children who think that once they've got guardianship over a parent with dementia or age-related memory loss they can take every asset and use it for themselves.'

'Gladys did not have dementia,' Gemma said tightly. 'She knew exactly what she was doing. Anyway, I didn't know a thing about what she had written in her will.'

'There are other even more disturbing cases where the elderly person is persuaded by a non-relative to hand over all of their assets or remake their will in their favour,' he said as if she hadn't spoken. 'Sometimes the person deliberately sets the elderly person against their family or even their lifelong partner. There was a case where a guy inveigled his way between a husband and wife who had been married for over fifty years. The husband was dying of cancer so this guy moved in and promised the old lady he would help with running their small farm. The family, who lived interstate, could do nothing as the old woman had acted while in control of her faculties. She continually handed over large sums of money to this guy until there was nothing left.'

'Just what exactly are you implying?' Gemma asked with a combative glare.

'I'm not implying anything,' he said. 'Everyone in town speaks very highly of you. You would be the last person anyone would suspect of devious motives.'

She folded her arms across her chest and sent him a cynical look. 'Apart from you.'

'I didn't say that.'

'I think you should find somewhere else to stay, Sergeant Di Angelo,' Gemma said dropping her arms to swing away to go back inside. 'You're no longer welcome here.'

Marc caught her arm on the way past, stalling her. 'Wait, Gemma.'

Gemma felt her skin tingle all the way up to her armpit as his fingers tightened to hold her securely. Heat rushed through her legs. She looked into his dark brown eyes and her belly turned over. His gaze moved from hers to her mouth and then back again. His tongue moved out over the dry landscape of his lips, signalling his desire to kiss her. She felt the tightening of the night air, the magnetism of his touch, how it drew her closer without her even knowing it. She felt the brush of his hard thighs first, and then the evidence of his growing arousal as the seconds throbbed past. His other hand had taken hold of her right arm as well as her left, his fingers like a pair of handcuffs around her wrists, his thumbs moving in a slow-moving caress that sent exploding fireworks of reaction down her spine. His eyes went to her mouth again, and then slowly his head began to come down…

'You're going to lose the bet,' she said, although her voice sounded like someone else's. It was husky and soft, breathy.

He paused just above her mouth, so close she could feel the subtle breeze of his breath on her parted lips. 'I haven't kissed you yet,' he said in an equally husky tone.

'No,' she said, running her tongue out over her bone-dry lips in a nervous, anticipatory gesture. 'But you were going to.'

He smiled a crooked half-smile that did serious

damage to Gemma's heart rate, quite possibly putting it in the training zone for the first time in several months. 'Maybe I will, maybe I won't,' he said, his thumbs still working their mesmerising magic on her wrists.

Go on, do it, Gemma silently pleaded. Her whole body was teetering on a precipice of longing to feel that sensual mouth commandeering hers. Her breasts were aching as they were pressed against his chest, her tight nipples abraded by the lace of her bra. Her stomach quivered with excitement. It had been so long since she had been kissed. Her lips trembled in expectation, with longing and heart-stopping need.

He slowly straightened and released her hands, stepping back from her. 'I guess I'd better go and pack my things,' he said, and made to go inside.

Gemma caught him by the arm, just as he had done to her only moments earlier. His forearm was warm and strong with lean corded muscles, the covering of masculine hair tickling her fingertips and palm. 'No,' she said softly. 'Please…please don't leave.'

One of his brows rose questioningly. 'You want me to stay?'

She moistened her lips again and lowered her gaze from the burning heat of his. 'I'm…I'm not asking you to sleep with me, Sergeant Di Angelo,' she said.

He tipped up her chin and looked deeply into her eyes. 'What are you asking me to do?'

She held his penetrating gaze. 'I'm asking you to trust me,' she said, 'to believe me incapable of exploiting an old woman for monetary gain.'

His eyes dropped to her mouth for a pulsing beat

before coming back to hers. 'Trust is an important issue for you, isn't it?' he asked.

'Yes, yes, it is,' she said.

He brushed his thumb over her bottom lip, making every nerve ending scream for more. 'You have a beautiful mouth, Gemma,' he said, 'just made for kissing.'

Then do it, for pity's sake!

'I could so easily lean down and kiss you,' he said, still caressing her bottom lip as his eyes held hers.

'What's stopping you?' she asked throatily.

He gave another one of his crooked half-smiles. 'I don't like losing.'

'Call off the bet, then,' she said.

He trailed a fingertip down the curve of her cheek. 'That's as good as losing in my book.'

'Are you always so good at self-control?' Gemma asked.

'I've trained myself to think beyond the heat of the moment,' he said. 'Self-control and discipline are hammered into us as cops. You can't lose control in a life-and-death situation.'

'This is hardly a life-and-death situation,' she said with a wry look.

'No, perhaps not,' he said, dropping his hands to his sides, a mask slipping over his features once more. 'You should go to bed. I'll clear this stuff away.'

'I thought I was the doctor and you were the guest,' Gemma said. 'Somehow today we seem to have switched places.'

'You're not used to having anyone to look after you, are you?' he asked.

Gemma looked away from his all-seeing gaze. 'I like

being independent,' she said. 'I figure I'm less likely to be let down that way.'

'Who let you down?' he asked. 'A lover?'

She looked out over the paddocks and to the ghostly silhouette of the willows down by the river. 'I had a fiancé back in Melbourne,' she said after a moment. 'He found someone else but forgot to tell me. I was still wearing his ring when she got pregnant. They're married now.'

'That would have been pretty tough to deal with.'

'It was, but I got over it.'

'Well done, you.' There was a touch of wryness to his tone.

She turned back around to face him. 'Maybe I will go to bed and let you clear things up down here. It's been a long day. Goodnight.'

'Gemma?'

She stopped in mid-stride and looked at him again. 'Yes?'

His eyes seemed to hold hers for an eon before he spoke. 'Why don't you call the bet off?' he asked.

Gemma felt a tremor of need rocket through her but she quickly squashed it. 'I'll think about it,' she said, and left him standing alone in the moonlight.

CHAPTER SIX

MARC had already left Huntingdon Lodge when Gemma came downstairs the following morning. She had taken the precaution of sleeping in one of the guest rooms rather than chance being disturbed by the mice again. She had slept fitfully, her head had ached a bit when she'd turned in her sleep, but the bruising was less noticeable this morning now she had covered it with some make-up. And thankfully she had heard no more squeaking.

Rob drove up the driveway as she was making a cup of tea. She waved to him as he got out and limped over to the house, taking off his akubra hat as he came indoors. 'I heard you got yourself punched,' he said, grimacing in empathy as he looked at the side of her forehead.

'It was my own fault for getting in the way,' Gemma said. Quickly changing the subject, she asked, 'Do you want a cuppa before you start on the hall?'

Rob gave his lower back a rub with one of his hands, his face screwing up in discomfort. 'Yeah, that'd be good.'

'Are you in a lot of pain today, Rob?'

'Same as usual,' he said.

Gemma felt for him. Chronic pain was debilitating and could affect mood and motivation. Rob was mostly stoic about it, but now and again he would seem depressed and lacking in focus. It didn't help that he had no partner or family to take his mind off his pain. He was only in his middle forties, far too young to be living like an old man. She knew he hated being on a pension. He had been born and bred on the land so to have to give up hard physical labour was like a blow to his masculine pride. She had prescribed painkillers from time to time for him but he often soldiered on without them, insisting he didn't want to become dependent on drugs.

'How long's the sergeant staying here with you?' Rob asked as he took the cup of tea Gemma had poured for him.

'I'm not entirely sure.'

'Seems a nice enough chap,' he said, and, winking at her, added, 'good-looking too.'

Gemma gave him a mock glare. 'If one more person says how nice it would be for me to hook up with Sergeant Di Angelo I swear I'll scream.'

'Speaking of screaming, the sergeant told me you heard a mouse behind the wall in your room,' Rob said. 'I put some poison in the attic and set a couple of traps in the cupboard under the stairs. I'll check on them before I leave.'

'Thanks, Rob,' she said. 'I really appreciate it. Oh, and thanks for bringing my car out last night.'

'That's all right,' he said, blowing on the surface of his tea to cool it down. 'Any news on Nick Goglin?'

'I called while I was waiting for Sergeant Di Angelo to drive me home from the clinic yesterday,' she said.

'He's still in a coma but some preliminary scans have offered some hope. It will be a while before we know what to expect in terms of recovery.'

'It's hard on Meg and the kids,' Rob said. 'Narelle mentioned you were planning some sort of charity-bash ball to raise some funds for her while Nick's out of action.'

'Yes, that's right,' Gemma said. 'I thought we could have a bush dance out here in the old shearing shed. All the shed needs is a good brush out with a broom and a few decorations. We can have a barbeque and a raffle of some sort.'

'Sounds good,' Rob said, putting his cup down. 'Well, I'd better get started on that hall.'

'Don't work too hard, Rob,' Gemma said when she saw him wince as he reached for his hat.

He twirled the brim round and round in his hands before he looked up to meet her gaze. 'It's not the same without her, is it?' he asked.

She put her cup down on the table. 'No, it's not,' she said softly.

Rob gave a deep sigh. 'I really miss the old bird. She was always so good to me. I sometimes wonder what I would have done without her over the years, especially since my father died.'

'She adored you, Rob,' Gemma said. 'Anyone could see that.'

He smiled a sad sort of smile. 'She was like a mother to me, Gemma. My own mother took off when I was four years old. What sort of mother does that to a little kid?'

'Oh, Rob, I didn't know that. How awful for you.'

'My dad and I had to do what we could to run the property,' he said. 'I know for a fact that's why my back's the way it is. I worked too hard as a kid. I didn't have a childhood, not really. I don't blame my dad, he was just trying to make ends meet by cutting down on labour costs. But in the end we had to sell off half our land to get the bank off our backs after the drought.'

'Have you ever seen your mother since she left?'

He shook his head. 'No, she took off with some travelling salesman and went to live in the city—Sydney, I think it was.'

Gemma felt for the little boy he had once been. She had lost her mother to a freak road accident and even though she had been well past childhood she still felt the loss keenly. How much worse to be left behind at such a young and tender age? No wonder Rob cut such a lonely figure at times. Worn down by pain and hurts that were decades old. 'Rob…' She hesitated and began to chew at her lip.

'I know what you're going to say,' Rob said.

'You do?'

'Gladys wanted you to have Huntingdon Lodge. She wanted to keep you here in Jingilly Creek. It was her way of making sure you never left us.'

'So she talked to you about it before she died?' Gemma asked with a frown of surprise.

'Not in so many words but I could see how much she longed for you to stay,' he said. 'It's what everyone wants. You belong here, Gemma.' He gave her a smile. 'Besides, if you sell up and leave I might not have a job to come to. The new owners might not want someone like me limping about the place.'

Gemma gave his arm a squeeze. 'I'm not going any time soon,' she said. 'Anyway, I have Flossie to think about, remember?'

Rob bent down and stroked the old dog's head. 'She misses her too, don't you, Floss?'

Gemma didn't get a chance to draw a breath before lunchtime. The clinic had been busy that morning with a rush of patients keen to get their flu vaccinations as well as one or two more seriously ill patients who needed some extra time with her to discuss their treatment options. But finally the last patient left and she was able to close the front door. She took a deep breath and walked to the small kitchen area where tea- and coffee-making facilities were set up, along with a microwave and toaster oven.

Narelle looked up as she came in. 'Poor Ellice is going downhill rapidly, isn't she?'

'Yes, she certainly is,' Gemma said, thinking of how devoted Ellice Peterson's family were to support her the way they did through her long battle with leukaemia. She had a particularly aggressive form that had resisted all forms of treatment. Ellice had decided to come home from her long stints in a Brisbane hospital to die in peace surrounded by the family she loved.

'You have something else on your mind,' Narelle said, regarding her with a musing look. 'I can always tell. What's up? Is the sexy sergeant getting too hot to handle? Don't tell me he's kissed you. Oh, my God, he has, hasn't he?'

Gemma felt that familiar rush of heat go through

her body whenever Marc's name was mentioned. 'No, of course not,' she said. 'Anyway, we made a bet.'

'A bet?' Narelle's eyes bugged. 'On what?'

'On not kissing each other,' Gemma said, flushing.

'I can't believe I'm hearing this.' Narelle gave the side of her head a couple of taps. 'You mean to tell me you made some sort of bet with Sergeant Marc Di Angelo over not kissing him? Are you out of your mind?'

Gemma set her mouth into a flat line. 'I had to put some sort of boundary up. He's living at Huntingdon with me for an unspecified time. It would be too easy to fall into a relationship just for the heck of it.'

'So?' Narelle said. 'Come on, Gemma, you haven't had a relationship since that jerk two-timed you back in Melbourne. Isn't it time to put that behind you and enjoy life a little bit?'

'Why is everyone so determined to run my life for me?' Gemma asked, reaching for a cup. It seemed there wasn't a person in the district who didn't think Marc Di Angelo was a perfect match for her. She'd had to field comments and ignore speculative looks all morning as each patient had wanted to know how she was getting on with the handsome city sergeant. She had enough trouble keeping him out of her head, without others reminding her constantly of how gorgeous he was and what an excellent husband he would make for her. She felt embarrassed that she was perceived as such a lonely heart. She hadn't realised she had been showing any outward signs of the deep inner yearnings she felt at times.

'Because we care about you, Gemma,' Narelle said. 'You do so much for this community but no one expects you to give up everything. You're entitled to have a life, you know.'

'I know. It's just that I'm not sure if I should make my life here or not.'

Narelle's hand froze on the cupboard door she had opened. 'You're not thinking of leaving us?'

Gemma bit her lip. 'I don't know…I feel so confused,' she said. 'I probably wouldn't have stayed this long if it hadn't been for Gladys, and now she's left me Huntingdon Lodge I'm worried it would look avaricious of me to suddenly sell up and leave.'

'I can understand how you would feel like that but you have to do what is right for you, Gemma,' Narelle said. 'Are you truly not happy out here?'

'Of course I'm happy here,' Gemma said. 'I love this place. You of all people know that.'

'But you still feel like you're missing something.'

'I guess I'm still trying to work out what I want,' Gemma said with yet another sigh.

'Aren't we all?' Narelle agreed as she handed over the chocolate biscuits.

The heat of the day had intensified rather than lessened by the time Gemma drove back to Huntingdon Lodge. There was no sign of Marc's car and Rob had already left for the day. The swimming hole was just the place to unwind. She put a bikini on under her trackpants and T-shirt and slipping her feet into sandals walked down to the river. Flossie had walked with her as far as the house gate but then gave an exhausted doggy sigh and returned to the house, away from the heat beating down on her thick coat.

The water was deep and cold and Gemma breathed out a long sigh of pure bliss as it covered her from head to foot. She surfaced to swim a few lengths of her makeshift pool, using the willow branches as a guide before she deftly turned back to go the other way. The sound of the water being shifted by her body and the gentle rustle of the breeze through the trees were a tonic for her after the difficulties of the last couple of days.

The alarm notes of a bird calling from the trees further along the bank made Gemma take pause. She trod water for a moment, peering through the limbs of the willows to see what had startled the bird.

Marc appeared from the dappled shade. He was wearing jeans and a T-shirt, which was damp and clinging to his chest from perspiration. Her heart gave a little stumble and her belly fluttered when he took off his sunglasses to lock his gaze on hers. 'This looks like the place to be on a day like this,' he said.

'How did you know I was here?' Gemma asked, keeping her legs moving under the water to stay afloat.

'I saw you just as I was turning into the driveway,' he said. 'How's the water?'

'Wet.'

His lips twitched. 'Fancy some company?'

Her eyes flicked briefly to his jeans-clad legs. 'Have you got bathers with you?'

'Do I need them?' he asked with an unfathomable look.

Gemma's belly did a flip turn similar to the one she had done only minutes before as she had swum back and forth. 'Um…I was about to get out anyway…' she said, making a move towards the bank.

'Don't let me spoil your fun,' he said, hauling his T-shirt over his head and tossing it onto a sun-warmed rock. 'It looks like there's room enough for two in there.'

Gemma's hands slipped off the reeds she had intended to use to get out of the water hole as his hands went to the fastener on his jeans. Her eyes flared and her heart rate went full throttle as she heard the metallic glide of his zip go down. He heeled off his shoes and pulled off his socks, and then he stepped out of his jeans. He was wearing close-fitting black underwear, the sort that left you in no doubt of how he was made. She had to grasp at a low-lying branch to keep herself afloat, her eyes feasting on him, devouring every delicious inch of him before he slipped into the water beside her.

'Mmm, that's better,' he said, before submerging completely.

Gemma kicked herself away from the bank, going to the middle of the water hole to give him some room.

When he surfaced right next to her, one of his legs brushed against hers under the water. It was the merest touch of flesh against flesh but it sent shockwaves of feeling right through her body. She moved backwards but he came too, treading water just in front of her, his dark eyes with their thick water-spiked lashes holding hers in a mesmerising lockdown. 'Do you fancy a race to the fourth willow and back?' he asked.

Gemma was nothing if not competitive. She felt her muscles already switching on for the challenge. 'Sure, why not?'

'You call the start,' he said, positioning himself level

alongside her. 'Do you want a couple of metres' head start?'

She gave him an are-you-kidding-me look. 'Ready, set, go!'

Of course, in the end he beat her easily, but Gemma gave it everything she had. It was exhilarating to fight it out stroke for stroke, metre for metre until he pulled away with a burst of speed and strength she had no match for. The light of victory shone in his eyes as he trod water near her and she noticed with annoyance his breathing rate had barely changed while she felt like her lungs were going to explode.

'Handicap next time?' he suggested.

'No way,' she said, trying to cover her gasping breathing. 'When I beat you, I'll do it fair and square.'

'You say that as if it's a given,' he said with a playful half-smile.

'Confidence is the key to success,' she said. 'If you think you can win something, you'll actively work towards it. If you think you're going to fail, it's like a self-fulfilling prophecy.'

His dark eyes took on a smouldering look as they held hers. 'So you haven't changed your mind about our little bet?'

Gemma put up her chin. 'Why should I have?'

His eyes flicked to her mouth, and then back to her gaze. 'Because I think we both want to take this one step further.'

Gemma felt her insides clench with desire, an on-off sensation that radiated out from her core. She ran the tip of her tongue out over her lips, tasting the brackish water and her own clamouring need for his kiss. Her eyes dropped to his mouth, her insides kicking again with excitement and anticipation as he too moistened his lips with his tongue.

It was a tense, enthralling moment.

Would he or wouldn't he?

Or would she throw caution to the winds and move forward and press her mouth to his sensual one just for the heck of it, just for the taste of it, just for the sheer thrill of having a man want her?

But then she remembered his arrogant confidence, his assurance that she would be the first to give in. She didn't like being that predictable. She gave him a coquettish smile and disappeared under the water, swimming away with strong underwater sculling and kicking motions.

When she resurfaced Marc was swimming with long leisurely strokes in the opposite direction. She swam over to the bank and climbed up on one of the larger rocks to watch him, her arms wrapped around her bent knees.

After a while he swam over and hauled himself out of the water with a lot more strength and grace than she had earlier, Gemma noted a little ruefully. She had the grazes on her knees to prove it. Water droplets from his body landed on her as he settled down beside her, his long, hair-roughened legs making hers look pale and milky in comparison.

'Hasn't anyone ever told you it's not advisable to swim alone?' he asked as he finger-combed his wet hair back off his face.

'I'm a capable swimmer.'

'Tree roots and submerged limbs make no allowances

for competence,' he said. 'You should always have someone with you.'

'You may not have noticed but there aren't too many lifeguards out here, Sergeant,' she said.

'Then the very least you should do is tell someone where you're going.'

'Once a cop, always a cop.'

'What's that supposed to mean?'

'You think it's your responsibility to keep everyone safe all the time,' Gemma said, resting the side of her face on one knee as she looked at him. 'Don't you ever switch off?'

'Do you?' There was a brooding intensity in his gaze as it collided with hers.

'I'm aware of the dangers of burning myself out,' she said after a tiny tense pause. 'It's one of the dangers of working in an isolated community. There's no downtime unless you actively seek it. Someone always needs you.'

He looked into the distance, his dark eyes narrowed against the slanting glare of the setting sun. After a long moment he got to his feet and reached for his clothes. 'We should get back before the mosquitoes start.'

Gemma stood up and went to where her clothes were lying. She got dressed and joined Marc on the path that led out of the willow glade. About halfway back to the house Marc's mobile rang and he took it out of the pocket of his jeans to answer it. She walked on ahead in case it was a personal call. Within a few minutes he had caught up to her, his expression grim as she turned to look at him. 'What's wrong?' she asked.

'Have you got your phone with you?'

'No, I left it at the house,' she said. 'Why? Is someone trying to contact me?'

'There's been an accident out at Jingilly gorge,' he said. 'A woman has fallen six metres. No one can get to her without abseiling equipment. The husband isn't sure if she's dead or alive.'

'Has the ambulance been called?' Gemma asked as she broke into a run.

'Ray's done that,' he said. 'They're already on their way. How far is the gorge from here?'

'Not far. We can be there in fifteen minutes, ten if we step on it.'

As soon as they got to the house Gemma grabbed her doctor's bag and joined Marc in his car. She gave him directions to the gorge and they drove out there with considerable speed, certainly faster than she would have done if she had been behind the wheel. Marc had put his portable siren on and the distinctive sound made Gemma's adrenalin surge all the more.

They arrived at the gorge just seconds before the ambulance. The husband of the victim was threatening to go down the rock face to rescue his young wife but Ray was doing his best to restrain him. 'Wait until we get the gear to bring her up, mate,' he said. 'The ambulance is here now and the doctor. Just stay calm, OK?'

The poor man was distraught, sobbing and tearing at his hair. 'We've only been married a week,' he choked. 'We're on a camping honeymoon. She was posing for a photo. I should have realised it wasn't safe. I tried to catch her but she slipped out of my hold.'

Gemma rushed over with her bag while Marc assessed the scene. 'I need to get down there to her,' she said. 'What are my chances?'

He let out a breath as he studied the terrain. 'Have you ever abseiled before?' he asked, swinging his gaze to hers.

'No, but if you've got the equipment I could probably give it a go,' she said, already feeling the flutter of nerves at the thought of going down that cliff face.

'I'll go down with you,' Marc said. 'But I think we'll need a chopper for the victim—that is, if she's still alive.'

Gemma swallowed as she looked down at the young woman lying in a crumpled heap so far below. 'How long has it been since she fell?' she asked.

'Half an hour,' Marc said, glancing towards the distraught husband, who was sitting on a log with his head in his hands.

'I'll call the chopper rescue just to be on the safe side,' she said, pulling out her phone and checking for a signal. 'It will take them time to get here in any case. Either way, it would be better if she was brought up via a winch.'

Marc didn't answer. He was already on his way to speak to Ray at the police vehicle, stopping briefly to place his hand on the bonnet of the husband's car, for what reason Gemma could not immediately fathom. Within a few minutes he had brought back some abseiling gear from the back of Ray's four-wheel drive. 'I'll help you down,' he said, uncoiling the ropes and assembling the clips.

It was a nerve-racking experience, going down the cliff, but with Marc by her side as Ray supervised the feed out of the equipment, Gemma felt as safe as anyone could feel given the circumstances. She bumped against the rocks a few times on the way down, but after a while she got the hang of using her feet to keep herself steady.

Feeling the solid ground under her feet when she finally made it to the bottom of the gorge was a relief, but she didn't have a moment to think about what she had just done. Marc had brought her doctor's bag down with him and handed it to her as they knelt beside the victim. The young woman, called Kate Barnes, was bleeding from a head wound and it was obvious from the unnatural angle of her right leg and left ankle that they were broken.

Gemma searched for a pulse and to her surprise and relief found a faint one. 'She's alive. You'd better let the husband know while I assess her condition,' she said, quickly donning gloves.

Marc called Ray on his phone, which seemed to Gemma a rather unusual thing to do when he could have just as easily given a shout to the top of the cliff face.

'How's she doing?' he asked as he came back and reached for gloves.

'Her airway is clear and breathing OK but I'm worried about that head wound,' Gemma said, as she worked on controlling the bleeding. 'She could have internal bleeding as well as a head injury. It's a heck of a long way to fall.'

'She must have broken the fall in a couple of places otherwise there's no way she could have survived that drop,' he said, glancing back up at the cliff.

'It's a miracle, that's for sure, but she's not out of the woods yet,' Gemma said as she went through her primary survey—airway clear, breathing twenty per minute, pulse about eighty, BP weak but palpable, GCS five or six, responding slightly to pain, exposure, possibly hypothermic. From her doctor's bag, Gemma retrieved a hard collar, adjusted it to small, and with Marc's help fitted it snugly to stabilise the neck. An oxygen cylinder, bag and mask were lowered down from the ambulance, with which Gemma was able to administer high-flow oxygen, with the patient breathing spontaneously. IV insertion came next, and a couple of bags of saline were lowered down in a bag from the ambulance supplies. Gemma's secondary survey had revealed an absent pulse in the right foot, certainly as a result of the tibial fracture above. She called for an inflatable splint from the ambulance, and had Marc stabilise the patient while she reduced the fracture and applied the splint, and breathed a sigh of relief at feeling the pulse return in the lower limb. Next a spine board was lowered, and with Marc's assistance the woman was carefully log-rolled onto it, sandbags coming down next and packed against each side of the neck. A space blanket was then applied to try to counter the hypothermia, and then it was a matter of maintaining oxygenation and circulation while waiting for the chopper.

The sound of the chopper arriving was an enormous relief. Gemma wasn't sure Kate was going to survive but her best chance would be to get her to Brisbane as soon as possible. While the chopper crew winched down the stretcher and a paramedic, Gemma was patched into the trauma centre via a handpiece to the chopper radio to fill them in on Kate's condition and vital signs.

It was almost dark by the time the chopper lifted Kate's shattered body up out of the gorge. Ray had set up some lighting from the top to guide Marc and Gemma back up, but it was a lot slower going up than going down.

'Don't look down,' Marc said at one point when Gemma froze when her foot lost its grip. 'Come on, sweetheart. You're doing great. Just keep looking at the next bit of the cliff. Concentrate on that.'

Gemma took a deep breath to control her panic. She felt beads of perspiration trickling down her shoulder blades, and her hands were sticky inside the climbing gloves Marc had given her to wear. Her heart was going like a piston. She felt dizzy and nauseous; terrified beyond anything she had ever felt.

'Come on, sweetheart,' Marc coaxed her again; his voice calm and soothing, just like a lover's. 'You can do it. One step at a time.'

'I can't do it,' she said, looking at him in despair. 'Marc, I don't think I can do it. It was so much easier going down.'

He bounced off the rock wall with his feet and held out his hand to her. 'That's because going down all you were thinking about was rescuing Kate,' he said with a smile. 'Come on, hold my hand. We'll go up together.'

Gemma slipped her trembling hand into the solid warm grasp of his, and slowly but surely he helped her to the top of the cliff face.

'Nice job,' he said, still holding her hand as she found her feet. 'I knew you could do it.'

'Sorry about the helpless female routine,' she said, giving him a sheepish look. 'I don't know what came over me. I just froze.'

'It was a tough climb for a beginner,' he said, releasing her hand and removing his helmet. He raked his fingers through his sweat-slicked hair before he helped Ray gather the equipment.

Ray came over to Gemma when the four wheel drive was loaded. 'I sent the husband, Jason, with the chopper,' he said. 'I thought he was going to go over that cliff as well.'

'What a dreadful thing to happen on your honeymoon,' she said. 'Are they from around here, do you know?'

'No, up from Sydney,' Ray said. 'Do you reckon she's going to survive?'

'It's hard to say,' Gemma said. 'She's got a pretty major head injury. But we got here pretty quickly so she's in with a much better chance than if it had been hours since she fell.'

Marc came to where they were standing. 'What time did you get the call from the husband, Ray?' he asked the junior constable.

'Five-thirty,' Ray answered. 'I was at the station when the call came through from the radio control room. I called you straight after. Then I tried both of Gemma's phones but she wasn't answering.'

'I forgot to take my mobile with me,' Gemma said, biting her lip.

'You can't be on call all the time,' Ray said. 'You work too damn hard as it is around here.'

'I'd like to interview the husband at some point,' Marc interjected. 'Did you get much of a statement from him?'

'Not much,' Ray said. 'He was barely coherent when I got here. I managed to establish that he and his wife pulled into the gorge just before five-thirty.'

'How did he react when you told him his wife was still alive?' Marc asked.

Gemma felt a ghost hand at the back of her neck. She wasn't sure where Marc was going with his line of enquiry. Did he really think Kate's fall hadn't been an accident? Was that why he had called Ray instead of shouting out, because he wanted to warn him to observe the husband's reaction? And was that why he had felt the warmth of the car on the way to collect the equipment?

'He was shocked but in a good way,' Ray said. 'The guy was beside himself. He was convinced she was dead. He was struck dumb with relief to find out she was still alive.'

Marc didn't answer. He had a look of concentration on his face as his dark gaze swept over the scene.

Gemma exchanged a quick glance with Ray but he just shrugged his shoulders in a beats-me gesture.

Marc had by now walked back over to where the couple's car was parked. He circled it a couple of times, crouching down to look at the pattern of footprints presumably. Gemma watched him move back to the edge of the cliff, shining his torch down over the area.

'What are you suggesting, Marc?' she asked when he came back to where she and Ray were standing.

'I want this place sealed off for a thorough investigation at first light,' he said. 'I'll get the Minnigarra guys in for back-up.'

Ray blinked as if he had missed something somewhere. 'What, so you think this wasn't an accident, Sarge?'

Marc gave him a grim look as he reached for his phone. 'I will decide that once all the evidence is examined, including the wife's statement, if she survives.'

'You think the husband…' Gemma gulped '…pushed her over the edge?'

'I think it's a possibility,' he said. 'That car's engine is stone cold. It was cold before we went down to do the retrieval. It's been here much longer than from five-thirty this afternoon.'

'You mean you think he…he waited before he called for help?' she asked. 'But why would he do that? If he wanted to kill her and make it look like an accident, why not just call for help as soon as he'd done the deed?'

Marc's expression was grave. 'Because he wanted to make sure she was already dead by the time help got here.' His mouth went tight before he added, 'That young woman was probably still conscious when she hit the ground.'

CHAPTER SEVEN

GEMMA hugged her arms around her body while she watched from the sidelines as the police from Minnigarra joined Marc and Ray as they worked on sealing the area. Two hours had passed since the chopper had left but there was no news on Kate's condition as yet. Gemma shivered in the cool night air as she thought about Marc's theory on what had actually happened. He was working tirelessly with the other officers, guiding them through the sophisticated investigation that would not have occurred without his powers of observation and mental acuity. She could see Ray was still trying to catch up, no doubt feeling a little out of his depth. The only criminal activity he'd had to deal with over the time he had been in Jingilly Creek had been the occasional robbery or drunken assault. Attempted murder was totally new territory for him.

Marc organised for the two officers from Minnigarra to stay on site and then he came over to where Gemma was waiting. 'I'll drive you home now,' he said. 'I'm sorry it's taken so long.'

'That's OK,' she said as she followed him to the car. 'Do you really think the husband pushed her? What if she just tripped and fell? It wouldn't be the first time.

We had a local boy break his leg here last year when he fell while throwing rocks into the gorge. He was lucky he was able to break his fall by grabbing one of the tree roots, but it was a near thing.'

'All possibilities will be examined,' he said as he opened the car door for her.

Gemma slipped into the seat and waited until he took his place behind the steering-wheel before she asked, 'What made you suspicious?'

He glanced at her as he gunned the engine. 'I'm a cop. It's my job to be suspicious.'

'But what if you're wrong?' she asked. 'That poor man will go through twice as much hell if he's wrongfully accused.'

'No one is accusing anyone of anything,' he said. 'I'm just looking at this from several angles. It's what I'm trained to do.'

'Ray didn't seem to think anything was untoward,' she pointed out. 'Neither did the Minnigarra officers.'

'I've worked in Homicide for close to a decade,' Marc said. 'I have a lot of experience in assessing situations like this. I'm not saying for a moment that Ray and the others aren't good cops. They just haven't had the level of experience I've had.'

'What will you do now?' she asked. 'Will you have to go to Brisbane to interview the husband?'

'I'll speak to my colleagues there and set up an interview to get an official statement from him,' he said. 'We'll have to do a check on his background. Find out if he has any priors, how long he's been married, what insurance policies he has taken out on the wife, that sort of thing.'

Gemma raised her brows at him. 'Wow, you really are amazingly cynical, aren't you?'

'Motive, Gemma,' he said as he turned the car towards Huntingdon Lodge. 'It's what you have to look for. I'm not always right. Sometimes things look suspicious but in the end turn out to be all above board.'

'Does that mean you might change your opinion on whether or not I influenced Gladys into leaving me her property?' she asked.

He met her gaze briefly before he turned the car in the direction of Huntingdon Lodge. 'You don't seem the type to exploit people for your own gain.'

'Are you going on gut feeling here or on evidence?' she asked.

He stopped at the cattle grid on the driveway, his gaze drifting over her in a smouldering manner. 'I haven't finished examining all the evidence,' he said. He sent the car over the grid and added, 'But I have a feeling it won't be long before I do.'

Gemma felt a tantalising little shiver race up her spine at his words. 'Are you flirting with me, Sergeant Di Angelo?' she asked.

A smile kicked up the corners of his mouth. 'Maybe.'

'What about the bet?' she asked.

'I'm not going to lose the bet.'

'You sound very confident.'

'I am.'

'Aren't you even a little bit tempted?' she asked.

He brought the car to a halt and looked at her. 'Are you?'

She pressed her lips together, not sure she wanted to admit just how tempted she was. 'Maybe.'

He got out of the car and came around to her side to open her door. Gemma got out on legs that suddenly felt like pipe cleaners. He closed the door with the flat of his hand but kept it there, like a blockade for her body. She felt the brush of his strongly muscled arm against her shoulder, every nerve in her body starting to tingle with anticipation. She sent the tip of her tongue out over her lips, watching him follow the movement with those dark melted-chocolate eyes of his. Her belly quivered like a partially set jelly as he put his other hand on the car on the other side of her body, enclosing her like a pair of brackets. 'Um…what are you doing?' she asked in a thready voice.

'How much have we got riding on this bet again?' he asked, looking down at her mouth the whole time he spoke.

She moistened her lips again. 'I don't think we came up with an actual figure.'

'So if I were to kiss you right now, it would only be my pride that would take a hit, not my wallet,' he said, still looking at her mouth.

Gemma's heart picked up its pace and her breathing became uneven. 'Some people value their pride more than their money,' she said.

His eyes met hers, holding them with searing heat. 'I have my share of pride but I wouldn't let it get in the way of me doing something I really wanted to do.' He moved closer, his lower body brushing against hers, setting off spot fires in her pelvis. He brought his mouth down, but not to her mouth, instead brushing his lips along the line of her jaw, a feather-light caress that sent a hot spurt of desire straight to her core.

'Um…isn't that a kiss of sorts?' she asked in a breathless voice.

'Believe me, sweetheart,' he drawled laconically, 'you'll know it when I kiss you.'

Gemma felt a shiver of delight ripple over her flesh. Her body was quivering with escalating need, her lips tingling for the press of his mouth. It was like a form of torture to have his mouth so close without possessing hers. Was he doing it deliberately to see if she would break the bet first? He moved in closer as he caressed the sensitive skin of her neck with his lips, and even at one point with the raspy tip of his tongue. She felt the hard bulge of his aroused body against her, the unmistakable signal of his desire for her, and her spine all but melted back against the car. 'Y-you're bending the rules,' she gasped.

'So book me,' he said gruffly, moving up to nibble on her earlobe.

He nudged her legs apart with one of his muscled thighs, imprinting his desire for her on her flesh until she forgot to breathe. She had never been so powerfully aware of her femininity, of her need and desire for a mate. It was a force beyond her control. It was an urge that had started with a slow burn but was now an inferno. She couldn't damp down the flames—they were licking through her at breakneck speed, consuming common sense in their wake.

In the end she didn't really know who lost the bet. She turned her head at the same time he did and somehow their lips met in the middle in a blaze of heat that spread through her body like wildfire. It was like an explosion, a combustion of built-up energy that consumed everything in its wake. She felt the skyrocketing of her pulse as he increased the pressure, his hands moving from where they were leaning on the car to slip behind her lower back and pull her closer. Her spine loosened, making her feel woolly and soft and limbless as his mouth continued its sensual feast on hers.

His tongue brushed across the seam of her lips and she gave a little whimpering sigh of submission as he drove through. His tongue probed and then darted, dancing with hers in a sexy tangle of growing need. He tasted so male and so delicious, unlike anything she had tasted before. It was like tasting a potent drug, and she couldn't get enough of him. Her arms looped around his neck as he moved even closer, his pelvis grinding against hers, the barrier of their clothes hardly a barrier for she could feel the pounding of his blood against her, the thickness of his body sending hers into a frenzy of want. He seemed to have unlocked something inside her. Now it had been let loose, she couldn't contain it. It was unbearable, unthinkable to stop, to pull back and act with the common sense and reason she had always prided herself on in the past.

He made a sound in the back of his throat, something between a growl and a groan, as she laced her fingers through his hair. His tongue swept over hers again, teasing it, cajoling it into another sexy tango that sent shivers trickling like a waterfall of champagne bubbles down her spine.

Her breasts tingled as they got crushed against the hard wall of his chest, the tight nipples pinpoints of sensation. A fire was burning between her legs. Hot sparks licking at her flesh, the network of sensitive nerves leaping and dancing and firing off in anticipation for more of his magical touch.

One of his hands moved from behind her back to cup her breast, a light touch, not tentative but neither was it possessive or grasping. It was experimental, exploring, and utterly irresistible. He brushed his thumb over her nipple, back and forth, sending another shockwave of feeling through her stunned body. How had her body survived this long without such heady pleasure? She ached to have him touch her without the barrier of clothes, to feel his warm fingers trace her contours, to feel his hot, masterful mouth sucking on her, drawing her into his sensual orbit.

Marc slowly drew back from her, holding her by the upper arms, his breathing not quite steady. 'Not sure who started that, are you?' he said.

Gemma gave him an arch look. 'You did.'

His mouth formed a rueful smile. 'Let's call it a draw, shall we?'

'We shouldn't have made such a stupid bet in the first place,' she said.

'Why?' he asked, his eyes glinting with something very male and very tempting. 'Because you knew right from the first day something like this would happen?'

Gemma pressed her lips together to stop them too from tingling, but if anything it made her more aware of how swollen and sensitive they were. 'It was just a kiss, Sergeant Di Angelo,' she said in a crisp tone. 'It's nothing to get too stirred up about.'

His hands moved from her arms to her wrists, his thumbs stroking her still leaping pulse. 'You think by switching back to the "Doctor" and "Sergeant" formalities, this will go away?' he asked.

Gemma swallowed as his warm breath caressed her face. 'It has to go away,' she said. 'We have to be sensible about this. We're both professionals in a small community. It could get tricky if we were to become involved.'

'Half the town thinks we already are involved,' he said as his eyes flicked down to her mouth as his head slowly lowered. 'May as well be hung for a sheep as well as a lamb, as they say.'

If she'd had any sense of self-respect or self-discipline, Gemma would have ducked out from under that tempting pressure and got away while she still could. But as soon as his mouth covered hers she was lost. She told herself it was because he was so darned good at it. He knew how to kiss with just the right amount of pressure, just the right amount of passionate intent to make her senses go into freefall. The heat inside her turned into a blaze of longing that sent hot, licking flames all over her body as each nerve reacted to his intimate embrace. His body was pressed up against her, his arousal so thick and strong she felt her spine wobble again as if someone had undone all her ligaments and tendons, leaving her vertebrae in a precarious house-of-cards pile that could topple at any moment.

He intensified the kiss, his mouth feeding hungrily off hers, making her realise with a little frisson of pleasure that he wasn't as in control as he had made out. She felt the tension in him building with each stab and thrust of his tongue against hers, the shockingly intimate mimic of what he really wanted. What she wanted. What their bodies both craved.

He lifted his mouth off hers, his breathing even more unsteady as he looked down at her. 'I really want to sleep with you,' he said. 'I want you in bed under me, on top of me, every which way I can have you. I think you need to know where I stand on that. I'm not the settling-down type. If we get involved, it will be an affair for a limited time.'

Gemma hesitated before she responded. She moistened her lips, caught in that moment of uncertainty she knew probably made her appear like a prudish relic from another time. 'You must think I am very out of touch.'

He picked up a stray strand of her hair and tucked it behind her ear. 'No, I don't think that at all,' he said. 'I think you are a nice girl who needs a man who can give you what you're looking for. I'm not that man.'

'How do you know what I'm looking for?' she asked.

His mouth went back into a rueful line. 'Sweetheart, what you want is normal—marriage and kids, the whole deal. I'm not interested in any of that for myself. You need to accept that.'

'Just because we kissed it doesn't mean I'm about to have you rushed off to be fitted for a morning suit,' Gemma said tetchily. 'Do you see every woman nudging thirty as some sort of ticking biological time bomb?'

He let out a long breath and scraped a hand through his hair. 'Look, I admit you pack a pretty awesome punch. I would love nothing more than a sizzling-hot affair with you. But within a month or two I'll be gone.

I don't plan to stay out here for ever. This is just an interim thing for me.'

'I'm surely adult enough to deal with it,' she said. 'If I wanted to indulge in an affair with you—which you are arrogantly assuming I do—then surely it's up to me to deal with the consequences when it ends, as it inevitably would.'

'I'm not arrogantly assuming anything, Gemma,' Marc said. 'I realise there is pressure on you from the locals to settle down because they want to keep you here. That is totally understandable because you're gorgeous and sweet and would make someone a fabulous wife. But I wouldn't want you or anyone else to get the wrong idea if we were to engage in a short-term relationship. It would be just that—an affair, not a promise of for ever.'

'Fine,' she said. 'I'll keep that in mind if I should be tempted to be so stupid as to agree to such a thing. Now, if you will excuse me, I need to go inside and have a shower.'

Gemma blasted herself with hot water but it did nothing to wash away her sense of shame at how easily Marc had read her heartfelt desires. She felt gauche and too country for his city sophistication. He obviously saw her as a homespun type, the almost-thirty-year-old spinster desperate for a suitable husband before the clock struck midnight, with the whole local community cheering her on from the sidelines. Argggh! How embarrassing! He was being sized up by everyone. No wonder he wanted to make things perfectly clear from the outset. He was used to slick city girls who went in for casual hook-ups.

He would not be interested in a woman who dreamed about sweet-smelling babies and a happy future with a man who loved and respected her.

She came downstairs only because hunger demanded it. There was Flossie to see to as well, not to mention her lodger, who would be expecting what exactly? Did he think she would agree to his no-string terms? Did he think her so needy and desperate she would gobble up the crumbs he tossed her way? She bit her lip as she searched the fridge for ingredients.

It would be so much easier if she wasn't tempted.

It would be so much easier if she had more experience.

It would be so much easier if she wasn't already halfway to being in love with him.

Gemma chopped onions with a savagery born out of frustration. The celery and carrots too were in for the same fate. Within minutes she had a stir-fry and rice on the simmer along with her temper.

Marc stepped into the kitchen. He too had showered and changed. His hair was still damp. It looked like glossy black satin and Gemma could see the track marks of his comb. 'Is there anything you would like me to do?' he asked.

'You can pour the wine if you like,' she said stiffly.

She heard the glug-glug-glug of the wine being poured into two glasses. She kept her head down, concentrating on keeping the ingredients from sticking on the bottom of the electric wok.

'Gemma.'

'Don't,' she said, looking up at him through a cloud of steam as she clanged the lid back in place.

He raised his brows a fraction. 'You're really angry.'

'Why would I be angry?' she asked, flashing him a quick glare from beneath her lashes.

'Why don't you tell me?'

She put down the wooden spoon on the bench next to the wok. 'I suppose you think I should be grateful that you've been so upfront about all this,' she said. 'I realise most men would have taken what was on offer and delivered the sorry-it's-me-not-you-speech later.'

'I'm just telling you it how it is, Gemma.'

'How can you be so confident you don't want what your parents and sisters have?' she asked. 'What makes you so different?'

Something flickered behind his dark gaze. 'I've never said I don't believe in marriage and family. I just don't want it for myself.'

She gave him a long, studied look. 'You know something, Sergeant? I don't believe you. I think you do want more for your life.'

'Stick to your day job, Dr Kendall,' he said with a curl of his lip as he reached for his glass. 'Leave the detective work to the experts.'

'I think that's why you're out here now,' she went on. 'You're at a crossroads. Why else would a hot-shot city sergeant come out here to this isolated community?'

A muscle beat like a pulse in his jaw. 'The same reason a city GP would come out, to do their bit for the bush.'

'I came out here to get over a broken heart,' Gemma said flatly. 'I was running away. Is that what you're doing, Marc?'

He put his glass down with meticulous precision,

and then his eyes hit hers. 'I have never run away from anything in my life,' he said. 'Now, if you'll excuse me, I have some work to do down at the station.'

She turned and frowned at him as he moved to the door. 'But what about dinner?'

'I'll get something later,' he said. 'Don't wait up. I have a key.'

Gemma let out a sigh as he strode out of the room. She heard his car roar as it started and then growl as it drove down the driveway. She looked down at Flossie, who was looking at her with empathy in her wise old eyes. 'You don't need to say I told you so, Flossie,' she said. 'I know I'm in over my head. I knew it the moment he walked into my consulting room. The thing is, what am I going to do about it?'

CHAPTER EIGHT

AS SOON as Gemma walked into the clinic Narelle raised her brows. 'Had a bit of a late night, did we?' she asked.

Gemma felt a blush steal over her cheeks. 'There was an accident out at the gorge. A woman fell six metres. We had to call in the chopper.'

'I heard about that from Ray,' Narelle said. 'But he said you were finished out there by nine, which kind of makes me wonder what you and the sexy sergeant got up to afterwards to give you those shadows under your eyes.'

'Nothing.'

'Liar,' Narelle said, leaning forward to peer at her. 'You kissed, didn't you?'

Gemma lifted her shoulder in a careless manner. 'So what if we did?'

Narelle's eyes bugged. 'Who lost the bet?'

'The jury's still out on that,' Gemma said. 'It sort of...happened.'

'So what was it like?'

'I'm not going to discuss such a personal thing with you, even if you are a close friend,' Gemma said.

Narelle gave a mock pout. 'Spoilsport.'

'Don't go ordering the invitations, Narelle,' Gemma said as she put her bag away. 'Sergeant Di Angelo has made his intentions clear. He isn't going to stay here for much longer than a month or two. This is just a fill-in post for him.'

Narelle clicked a ballpoint pen on and off. 'I wonder if he's had his heart broken,' she said. 'What do you reckon, Gemma? Perhaps he's come out here, like you did, to lick his wounds in private.'

Gemma frowned as she thought of the stony mask that had come over his face the evening before when she had pressed him about why he had taken the post. He hadn't even come back during the night. He hadn't even spoken to her by phone. Instead, he had sent her a text message early that morning saying he was going straight out to the gorge to continue the investigation into the accident. 'I don't know why he's here,' she said. 'But I do know it would be stupid of me to get my hopes up.'

'Ray thinks he's an excellent cop,' Narelle said. 'He said Marc put them all to shame with his assessment of the incident out at the gorge. No one was even thinking of anything suspicious until Marc put a red flag up.'

'I'm still not convinced it wasn't an accident,' Gemma said. 'The locals have been pushing for a safety fence ever since Jarrod Tenterfield broke his leg out there.'

'I know, but it can't hurt to ask some questions, can it?' Narelle said. 'If it wasn't an accident and this guy got away with it, think how awful that would be. Some other poor woman might have the same thing happen to her, or so Ray says.'

Gemma cocked her head. 'Since when have you and Ray been exchanging cosy little chats?' she asked.

This time it was Narelle's turn to blush. 'We're just friends,' she said. 'We've known each other for ever. Lyle and he used to be in the same class at school.'

'It's great that you've got someone to watch out for you,' Gemma said. 'Ray's a great guy.'

'I know but I don't want to rush things,' Narelle said. 'I have to consider Ben and Ruby. They still miss their father terribly. I don't want them to think I've forgotten all about him. I will never forget him, but he would want me to move on with my life. I would have wanted that for him if the tables were turned.'

'I'm happy for you, Narelle,' Gemma said as the clinic door opened with the arrival of the first patient. 'I hope it works out.'

Gemma was coming out of the bakery next to the general store at lunchtime when she saw Ron from the pub. 'Ron, I have a bone to pick with you,' she said, giving him a stern frown. 'I would have said something the other day but that drunken brawl distracted me.'

He grinned at her. 'What? Is Sergeant Di Angelo not paying his way?'

She narrowed her eyes at him. 'Do you realise how embarrassing this is?' she asked, lowering her voice in case anyone inside the bakery was listening. 'Everyone thinks we're having a relationship.'

'You could do a lot worse, Gemma,' Ron said. 'You never know, you might be able to change his mind about making his appointment here permanent.'

'I don't think so, Ron,' she said with a trace of despondency. 'He's not the small-town type.'

'Yeah, well, that's what you used to say but look at

you now,' Ron said. 'You're one of us. We can't do without you and you can't do without us. We're a team.'

Gemma chewed at her lip. 'Ron…I know everyone expects me to stay here for ever, especially since Gladys left me her property, but what if I did want to move back to the city at some point?'

Ron's bushy brows moved together. 'You're not thinking of leaving us?'

'I don't know…' She let out a sigh. 'Sometimes I wonder if I am missing out by staying out here.'

'You don't strike me as the flash restaurants and nightclub type, Gemma,' Ron said.

Just then a tall figure came across the road towards the bakery. Ron's weathered face broke into a grin. 'How's it going, Sarge?' he said. 'Is Gemma doing the right thing by you out at the lodge?'

Marc took off his police hat as he stepped onto the veranda. 'No complaints so far,' he said. 'She's gone out of her way to make me welcome.'

Gemma sent him a slit-eyed glare.

Ron just smiled and, tipping his hat at both of them, left to go back to the pub.

'Sorry I didn't make it back last night,' Marc said. 'I should have called you earlier to let you know.'

She raised her chin haughtily. 'It's no business of mine, Sergeant. You're a paying guest. You're free to come and go as you please.'

He scored a pathway through his thick hair with the fingers of one hand. 'I'm going to be away in Brisbane for a couple of days,' he said. 'I have an interview lined up with Kate Barnes's husband, Jason.'

'Is there any news on her condition?' Gemma asked.

'I should have phoned by now but I've been caught up all morning with patients at the clinic.'

'She's still in a coma,' he said. 'The doctors are still very guarded about her chances of surviving.'

'Has the husband given a formal statement?'

'Yes, but there are some inconsistencies with what we've found out at the gorge,' he said. 'I want to do some further investigation.'

'The locals have been pushing the Minnigarra council for a safety fence at the gorge for years,' Gemma said. 'If you ask me, it was an accident waiting to happen.'

His mouth lifted in a mocking smile. 'Still flying the innocent until proven guilty banner, eh, Gemma?'

She arched a brow at him. 'I thought that was your job as an officer of the law?'

His mouth lost its curve. 'It's my job to see the guilty are punished for their crimes.'

The door of the bakery opened and Marc stepped aside to let the person pass.

'Hello, Gemma, dear,' Maggie Innes said. 'Is this your handsome sergeant everyone is talking about?'

'Er…'

'Good afternoon, Sergeant,' Maggie said, beaming up at Marc. 'I can't tell you how excited we all are out here to have a fully qualified sergeant to look after us. How long are you staying with us?'

'I'm not sure,' Marc said. 'A month or two perhaps.'

Maggie's smile made her china-blue eyes twinkle. 'Maybe our gorgeous little Gemma will be able to change your mind. I believe you're staying out at the lodge with her. Is she a lovely hostess?'

'Very lovely,' he said.

'We're very proud of our Gemma,' Maggie said. 'She's the best doctor this place has ever had. We're terrified she might pack up and head back to the city. You'll have to collude with us to make her stay.'

'I'll do what I can,' he said, still with that deadpan expression.

Maggie gave them both a fingertip wave and waddled off in the direction of the general store.

'You've got yourself quite a fan club,' Marc said.

'Please don't feel under any obligation to join.'

He held her look for a beat or two. 'So what's in the bag?' he asked.

She put the paper bag she was carrying behind her back. 'Calories.'

He felt a smile tug at his mouth. 'How many?'

'Don't ask.' Her colour rose, making her look young and vulnerable, far too young and vulnerable for someone as jaded and cynical as him.

'I guess I'll see you when I get back,' he said after a noticeable pause. 'Is there anything you'd like me to bring back from the city?'

She shook her head. 'No, but thanks for asking.' She stepped down off the veranda. 'I have to go. I have patients waiting.'

Marc watched her walk back to the clinic, his eyes narrowed against the glare of the unforgiving sun. He waited until she had disappeared from sight before he let out a sigh that snagged on something deep inside his chest.

A week went past and Gemma heard nothing from Marc. Any news she had of the investigation over the fall at the gorge she'd got via Narelle, who had spoken to Ray. There had even been a couple of reports on the television news. Jason Barnes was under suspicion and had engaged a top-notch lawyer to defend his plea of innocence, and his family had rallied, offering up character references to clear his name. Gemma still couldn't decide what to believe about it all. It wasn't the first time a probably innocent person had been tried by the media, and the police didn't always get it right either.

The news on Nick Goglin was good but it would be quite some time before he would be back on the farm and able to work. The plans for the bush dance to raise funds to help the family were in full swing. In between seeing patients and a quick run out to Hindmarsh Downs to check on Elizabeth, Gemma put up flyers all over town about the fundraising dance. It was one of the things she loved most about living in such a small isolated community. Everyone chipped in to help each other. She had so many offers of donations of food and drink. Ron had donated beer and soft drinks and ice, and others such as Maggie Innes had offered to bake cakes and cookies for the supper. With Rob's help Gemma had cleaned out the shearing shed and Narelle and the kids had volunteered to help put up streamers and balloons for the event that coming Saturday.

On the Friday night before the dance Gemma was down putting the finishing touches to the shearing shed. Narelle and the children had left, which was probably why she hadn't registered the sound of a car pulling up. Even Flossie didn't prick up her ears, which gave Gemma absolutely no warning she was no longer alone.

She stepped back to survey her work and bumped

into a tall hard figure. Her heart leapt to her throat as she swung round, her chest heaving in panic until she realised it was Marc. 'You scared the living daylights out of me!' she gasped. 'Couldn't you have called out or something?'

'I thought you would have heard my car,' he said. 'I gave Narelle a toot on the horn at the gate when she was leaving.'

Gemma brushed a lank strand of hair out of her face. She felt dusty and dirty and dishevelled, and a little put out he hadn't made any contact with her, not even a text message to say when he would be back. 'I didn't realise you were coming back this evening,' she said, trying not to sound too churlish.

'I left a message on your landline,' he said. His gaze swept over the shearing shed. 'Nice job.'

'Thanks,' she said. 'It's been a lot of work but I think everyone is looking forward to it.'

'Do you need a hand with anything?'

'I was just going to move some of those hay bales closer for people to sit on,' she said pointing to a stack in the corner. 'Rob was supposed to help me but his back was playing up. I was going to get one of the men to do it tomorrow but as you're here now… That is, if you don't mind?'

'Not at all.' He put his keys down on one of the trestle tables Gemma had set up and got to work.

She watched as he lifted each bale as if it was a hand weight, positioning them around the area marked out as the dance floor. She could see the bunching of his muscles beneath his close-fitting T-shirt, each one taut and toned to perfection. Her belly gave a little shuffle as he came over to her once he had finished. He had some hay in his hair and dust on his shoulder. His eyes looked darker than normal, his thick lashes shielding his gaze as he looked down at her mouth. She felt the urge to moisten her lips but resisted it. She didn't want him to think her desperate for a repeat of their explosive kiss of a week ago.

'You have hay in your hair,' Marc said, and reached out a hand to retrieve it.

Gemma felt her scalp tingle at his touch, the slow drag of his fingers through her hair making her ache with want. 'You have too,' she said in a raspy voice.

His mouth kicked up at one corner. 'As long as I don't have it between my teeth,' he said. 'I can't quite see myself as a country yokel.'

She gave him a reproachful look. 'Is that how you see everyone who lives out in the bush?'

His eyes held hers in a little tussle. 'Don't get me wrong, Gemma. There are good people out here. I can see that. But I don't intend to stay around long enough to get too attached to the place. I'm a city boy born and bred.'

'I used to think the same thing,' Gemma said. 'I was determined I was only going to be out here for six months.'

'So why did you stay?' he asked.

She frowned as she thought about it. 'I don't know what or who changed my mind,' she said, kicking at a piece of hay on the floor. 'It was a gradual thing, I guess. I was hurting when I came out here. I thought my life was over. I couldn't see how my future was going to pan out without Stuart in it. We'd been together since med school.' She looked back up at him. 'I thought I was in love with him. I would have staked my life on it at the time but it was only after some time out here that I got some perspective. I had drifted into my engagement to Stuart. In fact, I don't think he even formally asked me. It was a sort of given. I was so used to us being a couple I gradually lost sight of who I was and what I wanted.'

'It can happen,' Marc said.

'Gladys was so lovely to me,' Gemma said. 'She was like a mother or really a grandmother, I suppose I should say. She helped me to see how much I had to offer in my own right. Having the responsibility of the practice really helped to build my professional confidence. It was something I never thought I would have been able to do. I would never have stretched myself in the city. It's too easy to send patients off to a specialist or for another opinion if you're not certain about a diagnosis or management. But out here I have had to deal with things I would never have seen in a city practice.'

'If you hadn't inherited Huntingdon Lodge from her, would you have gone back to the city by now?' he asked.

Gemma pressed her lips together before she answered. 'I'm not sure… Maybe. I think that's why she left it to me. She wanted me to take my time to think about it.'

'I can see there's quite a bit of pressure on you to stay,' Marc said. 'Everyone I have spoken to even in passing has told me what an asset you are to the place.'

She gave him a rueful look. 'The fan club.'

'Don't be embarrassed,' he said. 'It's a compliment to your dedication and commitment to the community.'

Gemma moved to straighten the paper cloth on the trestle table. 'Will you be coming to the dance tomorrow night or do you have other plans?' she asked. She turned and faced him again. 'Perhaps it won't be sophisticated enough for your city taste.'

His eyes stayed locked on hers for two heartbeats. 'I hate to tell you this but I have two left feet.'

She angled her head at him. 'I don't believe you.'

He held out his arms. 'Try me. I'll show you. I can't even do a waltz. Both of my sisters have tried to teach me over the years but I trod on their toes so much they quit in disgust.'

Gemma pushed her lips forward, wondering if it was a ruse. He was the most physically capable man she had ever met. 'All right,' she said stepping up to him. 'Put your hand in the small of my back. Yes, that's right. Now give me your other hand.' She covered her reaction but only just. His warm, broad palm felt like a hot pack against her skin, and the fingers of his other hand as they grasped hers radiated warmth up along her arm.

'There's no music,' he said as he moved in close to her body.

'We don't need music,' Gemma said as a shiver cascaded down her spine. 'Just concentrate on your own internal rhythm. Now, you lead with your left foot and I take a step back. That's it... Ouch!'

'Sorry, I did warn you about my feet.'

'Never mind,' she said. 'Let's try that again. Step, step, glide, step, step, glide and turn. Yes, that's better. I think you're getting it.'

They did a circuit of the shearing-shed dance floor. She got her toes stepped on a couple more times but after a while he seemed to get the hang of it and began to lead with more competence.

'How am I doing?' he asked against her ear as he expertly turned her.

'You're a very fast learner,' Gemma said. 'Do you want to try a barn dance now? It's not hard. You've already got the waltz part. There's just the progression section to learn.'

'I'm game if you are.'

'Right, then,' she said, positioning him to her left with right arm around the back of her shoulders. 'We take three steps forward and kick and then three steps backwards and then…'

It took a couple of attempts but he managed to get through the sequence without too much damage to her feet. 'Well done,' she said, smiling up at him. 'You have just officially graduated with flying colours from the Gemma Kendall School of Dance. Your sisters will be very proud of you.'

Marc was still holding her hands, his fingers warm and firm around hers. His eyes were dark, as dark as Gemma had ever seen them. She felt the magnetic pull of his body, the way it was drawing her closer to his hot, hard ridges and contours, even though he was standing rock steady.

The air suddenly tightened like a wire.

Then in slow motion his head came down, lower and lower until his warm breath skated over the surface of her lips in that immeasurable moment before he finally touched down, evoking a soft whimper of pleasure from her as his mouth sealed hers.

It was a dreamy kiss, the sort of kiss where she totally

forgot everything but the moment. The sheer sensation of having his lips move against hers, in tenderness and then with increasing pressure, as if something inside him that had been tightly controlled was slowly being unleashed. She felt it in the first stroke and glide of his tongue, the gentle urgency shifting up through the gears to full throttle want. His tongue danced with hers, but this was no slow waltz. This was a sexy tango that had an intimate progression in mind. She could feel the way his body spoke to her in the language of lovers, the aroused heat of him making longing seep through her body.

His hands moved from holding hers to gather her closer, one at the small of her back, the other cupping the curve of her cheek. The kiss went on and on, deeper and more sensual, drawing from her a response and need she had not known she was capable of.

His hand left her face to drift over the curve of her breast, a tentative touch, a teasing hint of how he wanted to explore her in more detail. She pressed herself against him, wanting more, aching for the cup of his palm and the caress of his fingers, the hot swirl of his tongue and the gentle nip of his teeth.

He walked her backwards in a parody of the dance steps she had taught him, one of his thighs moving between hers, tantalising her with its weight and strength, a potent reminder of how his body would feel driving inside hers.

Her back came up against the shearing-shed wall, the corrugations of the iron not unlike the ripples of feeling coursing through her. She kissed him back with wet, hot purpose, with hungry little nips and sucks of his bottom lip and greedy little pokes and darts with her tongue. She heard him groan as he pressed her up against the wall, his hands tugging at her shirt to free it from her jeans.

She felt the warm glide of his hand as it cupped her breast. Even through the lace of her bra it felt deliciously erotic, her nipple so tight it ached and burned. He bent his head and sucked on it through the flimsy fabric, the sensation of his hot mouth making her spine arch and her toes curl up inside her work boots.

He lifted his head and meshed his glittering gaze with hers. 'Do you want to finish this here or inside?' he asked.

Gemma suddenly realised what she was doing, or at least allowing him to do. She felt like a milkmaid being ravished by one of the farmhands.

A roll in the hay, so to speak. That was all it was to Marc. It was just another sexual encounter of which he had probably had hundreds. This wasn't about love or even liking. It was lust. There was no way of prettying it up.

He cocked an eyebrow questioningly. 'Gemma?'

She felt a blush moving up from her neck and had to shift her gaze. 'I'm sorry,' she said, ducking under his arm to put a safe distance between the temptation of his body and hers.

'Was it something I said?'

She bit her lip, wincing as it felt swollen and ravaged from his passionate kiss. 'I can't do this, Marc, not like this,' she said, waving her hand to encompass the rustic surroundings. 'It doesn't feel…right.'

'If you want roses and champagne then you'll have to move back to the city.'

'You don't strike me as a roses and champagne guy,' she threw back.

'You're right. I'm not.'

'I'm sorry for leading you on,' Gemma said after a tight silence. 'I got caught up in the moment. I've...I've never been kissed like that before.'

His eyes lost their hard glitter for a moment. 'It was a pretty awesome kiss, wasn't it?'

She felt a smile tug at her mouth. 'It was right up there.'

He smiled back, a lopsided half-smile that turned her insides over. 'You know something? I've never had a woman say no to me before.'

'My heart bleeds for you.'

He came up to her and slipped a hand beneath the curtain of her hair, locking his gaze with hers. 'Thanks for the dancing lesson.'

'You're welcome.'

His eyes flicked to her mouth and lingered there. 'I hope I didn't break any of your toes,' he said.

'No.' Only I think you might be well on your way to breaking my heart, Gemma thought.

His hand dropped from her nape as he took a step backwards. 'Have you had dinner?' he asked.

'No, but I can rustle up something for us,' she said. 'I'm just about done here.'

'I'll see you inside,' Marc said. 'I just have to get my things from the car.'

Flossie heaved herself up from the floor and limped over to follow him out into the night.

'Traitor,' Gemma said under her breath as she bent to pick up the wrinkled skin of a burst balloon that was not unlike how her chest felt right at that point.

CHAPTER NINE

GEMMA had a quiche and salad ready when Marc came downstairs after a shower. The homely feel to the kitchen, complete with elderly dog asleep on the floor under one of the chairs, clutched at his insides like a hand. It reminded him of his parents' house when he'd been growing up. It reminded him of Simon and Julie's house—before.

'Would you like a drink?' Gemma asked.

'Better not,' Marc said with a rueful look. 'I only just managed to control myself in the barn.'

Her cheeks turned a delicate shade of pink. 'I'm sorry…'

'Don't be.' He pulled out a chair.

She looked at him once they were both seated. 'How is the investigation going in Brisbane? I heard a few snippets on the news a day or so after it happened but nothing since.'

'Jason Barnes has lawyered up, as I suspected he would,' Marc said.

'But wouldn't anyone do that?' she asked. 'I know I would. I wouldn't want to be accused of something without having legal representation. People can twist your words and misquote you. It's too dangerous to go it alone.'

'Fair enough, but this guy has guilt written all over him,' Marc said. 'He took an insurance policy out on his wife three months before they married. They'd only been dating six months prior to that. She comes from a wealthy background. Loads of family money. Her parents are not keen to point the finger but one of her sisters spoke to Kate since the wedding and thought she was having some trouble with her marriage.'

'What sort of trouble?'

'Apparently Kate didn't say anything outright—it was just an impression the sister got at the time.'

'All marriages have a teething period,' Gemma said. 'Maybe Kate was just letting off steam.'

'Maybe,' Marc said.

'Have you ever got it wrong?' she asked, passing him the salad.

'Of course,' he said. 'Policing isn't an exact science. Even DNA can be planted—or contaminated. We have to be meticulous in investigating all lines of enquiry in an incident such as this. That's what really gets me about the bush. How many people are getting away with murder out here because of the lack of police or qualified officers conducting investigations?'

'Maybe you should think about extending your stay out here,' she suggested. 'Ray and the others could really learn from your experience.'

Marc frowned as he helped himself to salad. 'I've told the department a month, two at the most.'

'And you won't change your mind?'

'No,' he said, his expression closed. 'Why would I?'

She gave him a tight smile. 'Why indeed?'

Gemma let Marc clear away as she had to deal with a call from Janine Hindmarsh. Elizabeth had fallen and Janine was worried she had broken a rib or two. 'I'll come out and see her,' Gemma said.

'What, now?' Janine said. 'It's nearly ten at night.'

'That doesn't matter,' Gemma said. 'If she has hurt herself it would be best to get her to hospital sooner rather than later.'

'I feel terrible for putting you out like this.'

'Think nothing of it. I'll be there in twenty.'

Marc dried his hands on a tea-towel. 'Want some company?'

'How are you at handling difficult old ladies?' Gemma asked.

'I have a grandmother still living,' he said. 'She won't do anything for anyone else but she eats out of my hand. My sisters and mother hate me for it.'

'You're in.' Gemma tossed her keys to him.

As they drove out of the driveway, just to be on the safe side Gemma organised for the volunteer ambulance to join them at the homestead.

'Do you do this often?' Marc asked.

'What? Come out at night on calls?'

'It seems a big workload for one person.'

'I know but everyone pitches in out here,' Gemma said. 'My car broke down a while back and Joe Hindmarsh was the first on the scene to get me going again. It's how it works in the bush.'

'Here's your ambulance,' he said as a flash of lights

appeared in the rear-view mirror just as he turned into the Hindmarsh property.

After brief introductions were out of the way Gemma went straight to see Elizabeth, who was sitting in an awkward position in a recliner chair.

'I told you I'm all right,' the old woman grumbled. 'I wouldn't have fallen at all if it hadn't been for Janine leaving those boots near the back door. In my day I kept this place spotless. Not a thing out of place and everything in its place.'

Gemma exchanged a look with Janine, who was looking even wearier. 'Is Joe around?'

Janine shook her head. 'No, he's gone to Charleville to look at a new bull. He won't be back till tomorrow.'

'I think it might be best if we send Elizabeth to Roma for a few tests,' Gemma said. 'She might have fallen because of a TI.'

'You mean she might have had a stroke?' Janine asked.

'Only a minor one,' Gemma said. 'Elderly people with arterial sclerosis can have lots of mini-strokes without even realising it. They have funny turns, fall over or black out for a moment. It can be very upsetting, of course, and dangerous if they fall and hurt themselves.'

'I don't think she's going to agree to go to hospital,' Janine said, glancing at the stony-faced old woman sitting muttering in her chair.

'I'll see what I can do to convince her,' Gemma said. 'I'm concerned she might have broken a couple of ribs when she fell. She seemed rather tender when I examined her. And in any case, I think you could do with a few days of respite.'

'You mean you don't want me to go with her in the ambulance?' Janine asked.

'No, you stay here,' Gemma said. 'Dave and Malcolm can manage things between them. If you just pack a few of her things—a nightgown or two and her toiletries bag—that would be great.'

After a volley of protestations that got more and more vitriolic, Elizabeth Hindmarsh was finally loaded into the back of the ambulance, but only after Marc took control. He handled the old woman like a dream, charming her into agreeing that the best place for her was hospital, where she could be looked after around the clock.

'Don't know how you did that, mate,' Dave said as he closed the door of the ambulance.

'Piece of cake,' Marc said dryly.

'You owe me for this, Gemma,' Dave said as he took his place behind the wheel, with Malcolm riding shotgun.

Gemma smiled sweetly. 'Have a nice trip.'

Janine was all for offering them supper, but Gemma didn't want to expose Marc to any more obvious attempts at matchmaking. She could see the way Janine's eyes had been dancing with delight from the moment Marc had stepped into the homestead.

'Thanks, Janine, but it's late and we really should be in bed,' Gemma said, and then blushed to the roots of her hair. 'I mean, he should be in his bed and I should be in mine.'

Janine smiled a wide smile. 'How are you enjoying staying at Huntingdon Lodge, Sergeant Di Angelo?'

'I'm having a great time,' he said with a glinting smile. 'Gemma's even given me dancing lessons.'

Janine's brows lifted. 'Has she now? How delightful. So you'll be at the bush dance tomorrow night?'

'Wild horses couldn't keep me away,' he said.

Gemma rolled her eyes at him on the way to the car. 'Do you realise what you've just done?' she asked.

'Pardon me, sweetheart, but you were the one who was talking about going home to bed,' he pointed out wryly.

'A mere slip of the tongue,' she said, wrenching the door open. She glared at him over the roof of the car. 'You might as well have broadcast it all over town that we…that we…'

'That we what?'

'Never mind.' She got in and shut the door, frowning crossly.

'You worry too much about what people think,' Marc said as he drove out of the property. 'So what if you have a red-hot affair with a fly-in?'

'That's exactly my point,' Gemma said. 'I'm not looking for something temporary or casual. I'm not built that way.'

'What? So you're going to spend the rest of your life out here in this dead-end town, waiting until Mr Ticks-All-The-Boxes-For-You comes along?' he asked. 'Come on, Gemma. Get into the real world. You're going to throw your life away before you know it.'

'I could say the same about you,' she tossed back.

He shot her a cutting look. 'I'm fine with my life just the way it is.'

'Sure you are,' she said, folding her arms across her body. 'Flitting in and out of casual hook-ups with no promises of commitment, no lasting love, no kids and no growing old together. Yes, I can see how that could work for you.'

'You don't know what the hell you're talking about,' he muttered darkly.

'I do know,' Gemma said. 'I see couples out here who have lived their entire lives together. They've lived through heartbreak and happiness, all the highs and lows of life, and yet they've survived and stayed together. That is what life is about. It's not about living as an individual. It's about relationships. It's about community.'

'Not everyone survives,' he said. 'Not everyone gets their happy-ever-after.'

'I know that,' Gemma said. 'But that's where other relationships count. They support you through those rough times.'

'Good luck with it, Gemma,' he said. 'I hope you get what you want. I really do.'

I hope so too, Gemma thought dispiritedly.

Marc left early the next morning to do the day shift at the station. He had been up and gone for a run even before Gemma got out of bed. They crossed paths over breakfast but he didn't hang around for idle chit-chat. He seemed preoccupied and restless but, then, so was she. She had spent a couple of hours lying awake the previous night thinking about him, wondering if she had burned her bridges by rejecting his offer of a short-term affair. She had heard him moving about his room as if he too hadn't been able to sleep. Would it be so wrong to indulge in a steamy liaison, even if it didn't last? Was she being too much of an idealist, waiting for all the planets to align? Would she regret this one day in the future? Marc thought she was in danger of throwing away her life out here in the bush. She worried about that too.

It had never been in her plans to stay out here indefinitely. But what was to say her life would be any more fulfilling back in the city? She had a sense of purpose out here. She belonged to a much larger family than her own. It was a nice feeling to be needed and appreciated, but would it be enough to satisfy her in the longer term?

Marc hadn't yet returned when the first of the cars arrived. Gemma welcomed everyone and handed around food and drinks while Ron, Rob and Ray organised the music system. After a few hiccups the music started to pump out of the speakers and several couples got up to dance.

'I see the three Rs have got things under control,' Narelle said to Gemma as she passed around a platter of cheese cubes, olives and home-made pickled onions.

Gemma smiled. 'Yes, thank God for testosterone.'

'Speaking of which, where is your Marc?'

Her smile faded. 'He's not my Marc.'

'Not progressed past kissing, then, huh?' Narelle asked.

'I don't want to talk about it.'

'Ah, here he is now,' Narelle said, nodding towards the shearing-shed door. 'If you don't ask him to dance, I will.'

'He'll crush your toes,' Gemma warned.

'It'll be worth it,' Narelle said, and sashayed off with her tray of nibbles.

Gemma turned away to help serve some drinks to the children who had accompanied their parents. 'Here you go, Amy,' she said to the blond-haired five-year-old who had eyes as blue as the summer sky.

'Fanks,' the little girl said shyly.

'Does the new sergeant have a real gun?' Thomas Bentwood, Amy's older brother, asked as Gemma poured him some orangeade.

Gemma was wondering how best to answer when Marc appeared at the drinks table. 'Um… Hi,' she said. 'Thomas and Amy, this is Sergeant Di Angelo. Sergeant, this is Thomas and Amy Bentwood.'

Thomas put out his hand and after a brief hesitation Marc took it and gave it a solemn shake. 'Nice to meet you, Thomas,' he said. He smiled at Amy. 'You too, Amy. That's a really pretty dress you're wearing.'

'It's new,' Amy said proudly. 'My mummy made it for me specially.'

'Have you ever killed anyone?' Thomas asked Marc.

Gemma saw a flicker of something pass through Marc's eyes but he covered it quickly. His smile as he looked down at the children seemed a little forced, however. 'Not intentionally,' he said. 'But sometimes police officers have to do things they would prefer not to do in order to keep other people safe.'

'I want to be a policeman when I grow up,' Thomas said. 'I want to shoot people.' He shaped his hand like a gun and aiming it at his sister said, 'Bang, bang, you're dead.'

'Thomas.' Gemma laid a gentle hand on the eight-year-old's shoulder. 'Why don't you take your sister over to Mrs Innes's cupcakes stall? I think I saw her with some lolly bags earlier.'

The children scampered off and Gemma looked up at Marc. 'Kids,' she said.

'Yeah.' He thrust his hands in his jeans and surveyed the couples on the dance floor for a long moment. 'You've got a good turnout.'

'Yes, I think just about everyone in town is here,' she said. 'It'll be a good chance for you to meet everyone.'

He swung his gaze back to her. 'I suppose I should ask you to dance.'

She gave him a churlish look. 'No one is twisting your arm.'

His lips twitched. 'I'd like to. I want to make sure I can still do it, with the music this time.'

'I'm sure you'll be fine,' Gemma said. 'It's like riding a bike.'

'You reckon?'

She smiled as he took her hand and led her to the dance floor. 'Just keep your big clumsy feet away from mine,' she said, and melted into his arms.

Gemma knew everyone was watching them but somehow it didn't matter. Being in Marc's arms was an experience she wanted to savour for as long as she could. She was finding it harder and harder to think of reasons why she shouldn't take things to the next level. For her it was not so much about lust. It was ironic that she had dated Stuart for years without being entirely certain of her feelings for him, and yet with Marc it had only been a matter of days and she felt her love for him blossoming like a flower opening to the sun.

'How am I doing?' Marc asked as he weaved them out of the way of another couple.

'Impressive,' Gemma said. 'You've only stepped on my toes once.'

'There's hope for me yet.'

'Hey, can I steal your partner, Sarge?' Rob asked as he approached them. 'Sorry, Gemma, but one of the kids has taken a tumble outside. I thought you might want to check it out.'

'Sure,' she said, slipping out of Marc's hold. 'Who is it and what happened?'

'Young Matthew Avery,' Rob said. 'You know what a daredevil he is. He jumped off the top of the tank and gave himself a gash in the leg.'

Gemma went to the young boy, who was putting on a very brave front. There was a lot of blood but on examination it looked as if a couple of stitches would soon sort things out. Marc carried him inside for her and she set up her equipment in one of the downstairs rooms.

Matthew's mother came in, carrying her youngest on her hip, her other tearaway son's hand clasped firmly in her other hand. 'What's he done now?' she asked wearily.

'Nothing too serious,' Gemma said. 'I'll pop a couple of stitches in and if you bring him to see me on Monday I'll check that all is going as it should.'

The wound was soon attended to and Matthew and his mother went back outside to the shearing shed, Matthew proudly showing off his starkly white bandage on his tanned shin.

'Do you ever get a break out here?' Marc asked as Gemma cleared away the dressings and swabs. 'You seem to be at everyone's beck and call all the time.'

'I guess I'm used to it now,' Gemma said. 'At first I was a bit taken aback by the kerbside consultations, but after a while I realised it was because I was accepted by everyone. They feel comfortable approaching me. I like that. It makes me feel needed.'

'You should set some limits,' he said, frowning. 'You'll burn out before your time.'

'I was thinking about taking a holiday when Gladys got sick,' she said. 'Now with Flossie to take care of, I've had to rethink my time frame.'

'Where were you planning on going?'

She straightened the cover on the bed. 'I hadn't really got that far. I guess somewhere where there's a beach and those fancy cocktails with an umbrella and tropical fruit on a stick in the glass.'

'You're making me drool,' he said.

Gemma smiled. 'When was your last holiday?'

'I took a month off late last year. I visited my sister in Sicily and then I did a bit of a tour around Europe.'

'Did you go alone?'

'That's the best way to travel, in my opinion. You get to do what you want when you want. No detours to look at stuff that is of no interest to you.'

'Have you always been such a lone wolf, Marc?' she asked.

His expression became shuttered. 'We should get back to the dance,' he said, holding the door for her.

She held his look for a moment. 'Tell me what happened, Marc. Tell me what happened to you to make you lock yourself away from everyone.'

His jaw tensed, making the edges of his mouth whiten. 'Leave it, Gemma,' he said. 'Just leave it, OK?'

She let out a sigh as he strode out of the room ahead of her, his long, strong back like a drawbridge pulled up on the moat of the emotions she had caught a glimpse of earlier. Just what lay at the bottom of that deep, dark moat that haunted him so much?

The bush dance was declared a fabulous success. Several hundred dollars had been raised and promises of more support for Nick and Meg and the kids were assured as the night drew to a close. Gemma hadn't seen much of Marc since he had left her earlier. She wondered if he had made himself scarce so as not to intimidate the more enthusiastic revellers who were enjoying a last beer or two before they headed home. She had seen Ray cautioning a couple of the men about driving under the influence, but mostly everyone had acted responsibly.

Gemma was tidying up the kitchen at close to one in the morning when Marc came in from outside. 'Oh, I thought you must have gone to bed or something,' she said. 'I haven't seen you around.'

'I went for a walk,' he said, picking up a fresh glass and pouring in some wine from an opened bottle.

She gave the bench another wipe, her eyes downcast. 'I hope I didn't upset you earlier,' she said. 'I was probably stepping over the line with the trust-me-I'm-a-doctor routine. I'm so used to people telling me all their stuff I didn't respect your need for privacy.'

'It's OK,' Marc said taking a sip of the wine before putting it down on the bench.

She turned and faced him. 'No, really, Marc, I'm sorry. It's none of my business what's going on in your life.'

Marc looked at his glass but pushed it away rather than picking it up again. There had been a time when the only way he'd been able to block out his past had been to down glass after glass of alcohol. It hadn't made it any easier. It hadn't absolved his guilt. It hadn't taken Simon's wife Julie's shattered expression out of his head, neither had it taken the lost and bewildered look of Simon's little boy Sam, who had been used to his father bringing Marc home with him for a meal after a shift. Arriving that evening to tell Julie and Sam that Simon was not coming home had been the hardest thing he had ever had to do. Ever since the funeral he'd barely been able to bring himself to visit them. Just to be reminded of all they had lost and how he had lost it for them was too hard for him to face. His superiors had stepped in by giving him an ultimatum. He'd taken it because he'd wanted to see if he could still be a good cop. It was his life, his calling, and yet there were times when he wondered if he still had what it took.

'Marc?' Gemma's soft voice brought his head up and his eyes to her grey-blue ones.

'I watched my best mate get gunned down in front of me,' he said. 'We were on a job. I was heading the operation. Simon was following my orders when he lost his life. I can never forgive myself that it was him and not me in the way of that bullet.'

Her face fell. 'Oh, Marc…'

'Simon's wife and son have lost their world,' he said. 'One day they were a happy family unit and the next it was ripped away from them. Sam will grow up without a father, Julie without the husband she'd loved since she was a schoolgirl.'

'It wasn't your fault,' Gemma said. 'You can't blame yourself. You didn't fire the bullet.'

He gave her the humourless movement of his lips that had lately become his way of smiling. 'No, I know that. The guy who did it is locked away for life but it doesn't make it any easier. I've been given a life sentence too.'

Gemma came around to his side of the bench and laid her hand on his arm. 'You're the one who's given yourself a life sentence,' she said. 'You're denying yourself as a way to punish yourself. Surely Simon wouldn't have wanted you to do that. Would you have wanted him to do that if things had turned out the other way around?'

Marc looked at the soft bow of her mouth. Kissing her had been a big mistake. He had crossed the line and it couldn't be uncrossed. She wasn't like the other women he had been involved with in the past. She had an air of fresh innocence about her that was engaging and delightful. He thought of all the jaded types he had lost himself in for brief moments of physical release. He could barely recall their names. Not one of them had made his body throb with such heady desire after sharing just a kiss. He could feel it even now; the way his lips still tingled from being pressed to her mouth, even though more than twenty-four hours had passed. She had tasted unlike any other woman he had kissed and he had kissed plenty.

Gemma had tasted of strawberries and warm summer nights, of sunsets and sun-showers. It was a shock to realise how much he wanted to kiss her again. How he wanted to feel that electrifying passion again and again. But kissing her wasn't enough. He wanted more than that. He wanted to feel his body moving within hers, taking them both to paradise.

He laid his hand over hers, his darker skin making hers appear all the lighter. He felt the nervous flutter of her pulse and a wild stallion kicked him in the groin. 'God, I didn't want this to happen,' he said, bringing her towards him.

She softened like butter under the glow of a blowtorch as she came to him. His body kick-started against her, the leap of his pulse and the rocket fuel of his blood as it surged through his veins sending his rational mind to some far-off place way out of his reach. His mouth came down hard on hers, his nostrils flaring as he breathed in the scent of her and his tongue relishing the exquisite taste of her as the kiss went on and on and on. She moved against him in an instinctive request, a silent plea for the pleasure she was seeking from him and him from her.

It was an unstoppable force that had captivated them both. Long, tight, hot wires of need coiled around them, pulling them closer and closer. His body, her body, the combined heat and need lifting the hairs on his scalp as he thought of sinking into her. It was what he wanted. It was what she wanted. It was pointless trying to resist. They were both adults. They were old enough and responsible enough to take what they wanted without anyone getting hurt.

Gemma lost herself in his drugging kiss. If anything, it was even more sizzling and heart-stopping than the previous ones. She felt it in the way he pressed his mouth against hers, taking his time, not using his tongue until she opened her mouth to him on a breathless little gasp. It was like lightning striking when his tongue curled around hers. She even jolted against his body, her nerves singing in reaction as he deepened the kiss. He kissed her hungrily, passionately, purposefully, as if he had come to some decision in his head about her that he was not quite ready to put into words. The kiss went on and on, ramping up her desire for him inexorably. She felt the moistening of her body, the intimate dew of feminine desire in response to her mate. Her breasts too were tight and aching with need, the sensitive nipples tortured by the hard plane of his chest as he held her to him with hot, hard urgency.

He wrenched his mouth off hers and looked down at her with eyes glazed with heat and longing. 'This is madness,' he said. 'I don't know what it is about you but I can't seem to keep my hands off you.'

'It's just lust,' Gemma said a little breathlessly. 'It happens.'

He brought his hands up to her cheeks, cupping her face with the broad span of his fingers. 'You're a nice girl, Gemma,' he said, resting his forehead for a moment on hers. 'I don't usually sleep with nice girls.'

'Then maybe it's time you took a walk on the mild side,' she quipped.

'There,' he said, pulling back to look at her. 'That's why you stop me in my tracks. You're smart and funny. I don't think I've ever met anyone quite like you before.'

'That sounds like a line.'

His mouth twisted. 'It does, doesn't it?'

Gemma looked at him for a long moment, coming to her own decision. 'Marc, I…'

He put a finger to her lips. 'Don't say it.'

'Bufftt.'

'We're practically strangers,' he went on, keeping her protests muffled against his finger. 'I don't want to give you false hope or mislead you in any way. I want you to know exactly where you stand and where I stand.'

Gemma pushed her tongue against his finger, watching as his eyes flared with another wave of need. 'Will you shut up and make love to me, for pity's sake?' she asked.

His eyes burned with heat as they locked on hers. 'That, Dr Kendall,' he said as he lifted her in his arms, 'will be my very great pleasure.'

Marc carried her to his bedroom, shouldering open the door and dropping her on the bed with urgency rather than finesse. She lay there looking all feminine and soft and dewy-eyed and his groin gave him another zap of longing. He couldn't think of a time when he'd wanted someone more than her. It was like a fire in the river of his veins; they surged and pumped with it, sweeping away all sense and reason. He tore off his T-shirt and heeled himself out of his shoes before putting his hands to the waistband of his jeans. She was still lying there, looking up at him with a soft little smile playing about her mouth, but her chest was rising and falling at much the same hectic rate as his. 'You sure you want to take it this far?' he asked.

She looked him square in the eye. 'I'm sure.'

He dropped his jeans but kept his underwear on. He came over to her and lay down on the bed, half over her, his body leaping in excitement when her legs opened to make room for him. 'You're beautiful,' he said, lifting up the curtain of her hair to kiss her scented neck.

She turned her head so her mouth could find his, her soft lips parting as he drove through with his tongue. She tasted so damn good, so sweet and fresh he had trouble keeping his head. It was like making love for the first time. Everything felt so new and exciting: the touch of her hands as she explored his chest; the way her fingertips danced over him, brushing over his flat nipples before moving up to thread through his hair.

Marc gently worked on her clothes, taking his time over it, relishing every time another part of her was exposed to his vision. She had glorious skin, creamy and soft, just kissed by the sun, not burnt or heavily tanned.

He brought his mouth to the curve of her lace-clad breast, sucking on it through the delicate fabric, delighting in the way she arched under him at his touch. 'You like that?' he asked.

She answered him with a hot, moist kiss that nearly took the top of his head off. He tangled his tongue with hers, duelling with it, teasing it until she was moving beneath him restlessly.

He deftly removed her bra and feasted his eyes on her small but perfectly shaped breasts. They felt so soft to his touch, so feminine and delicate with their rosy pink peaks. He took each one in his mouth by turn, enjoying the way she melted as he worked his tongue around each nipple until it was as tight and erect as its twin.

He moved down her body, kissing her sternum, each side of her ribcage and then the shallow pool of her belly button. She arched up again and he settled her with a hand on her hip. 'Relax, sweetheart,' he said. 'I'm not going to rush you.'

She made a soft whimpering sound as he kissed her through the lace of her matching knickers. She was so responsive it made him feel as if he was in totally new territory. She moved against his hand when he peeled back the lace shielding her, her body asking him for more.

He gave it.

He parted her gently and explored the humid heart of her, the scent of her filling his senses. He brought his mouth down, tasting her, teasing her with his lips and tongue until she was gasping out little breathless sobs of release.

'I didn't… I thought… I haven't…' She blushed when his eyes met hers.

Marc stroked a long finger down her cherry-red cheek. 'You're not a virgin, are you?'

'No, it's just that I haven't done that… I mean, it didn't feel right…before now…' Her eyes fell away from his.

He tipped up her chin to make them come back to his. 'Hey, that's not something to be embarrassed about. Sex is all about chemistry. What feels right for one couple won't be right for another.'

She compressed her lips for a moment. 'I expect you're much more experienced than I am.'

'Is that a problem?' he asked.

'No, of course not.' She chewed at her bottom lip, this time reminding him of a shy child who was way out of her depth and knew it.

He brushed his thumb like a paintbrush over her lip where her teeth had left an indentation. 'I always practise safe sex,' he said. 'Is that what is worrying you?'

'I'm not worried,' she said, but he wondered if that was true.

'We don't have to go through with this if you're not ready,' Marc said, easing off her.

She grasped at his forearms to stop him from moving away. 'Don't go...please?'

He held her grey-blue gaze for a beat or two. 'I want you,' he said. 'I don't think I've ever wanted someone as much as I want you. Does that sound like a hackneyed line to you?'

She linked her arms around his neck and brought his head down. 'It sounds wonderful to me,' she said, and pressed her soft mouth against his.

This time there was no stopping him. Marc felt the rush of his blood as she tugged at his underwear, her fingers soft but worshipful as they uncovered him. He sucked in a breath as she curled her fingers around his length, the pressure of her grip just right. He reached past her to find a condom in the drawer where he had left his wallet and his gun. It was a bit of an effort but she was keeping herself busy in the meantime. He came back with the foil packet and got it on before she took him over the edge.

That first thrust, gentle as it was, took him totally by surprise. The feeling of her slim, tight body clenching around him, welcoming him into her, was mind-blowing. He increased his pace, slowly, careful not to rush her, but the control it took was costly. She was keeping up though with soft little gasps of pleasure as his body moved within hers, delighting him anew. He played her with his fingers, softly, coaxing her back towards paradise and she came willingly and enthusiastically. Her ripples of release triggered the switch on his control, and with a burst of blinding white light he emptied himself, collapsing as if he had run a marathon when it was over.

Her hands danced over his back and shoulders, her soft fingertips like fairy feet as she explored the knobs of his vertebrae. She moved up to curl her fingers in the back of his hair, tugging and stroking until he felt his skin pepper in goose-bumps of sensory pleasure. He felt her press a soft-as-air kiss to his jaw, then to his cheek and then she went in search of his mouth.

He met her more than halfway, drowning again in the damp heat of her lips and shy but still playful tongue. Her lips felt swollen beneath his and he eased off the pressure, realising it had been a while since they had been subjected to this degree of attention. How long he wasn't quite sure. He didn't really want to know. He didn't want to think of where this would go, or could go. This was here and now and it felt good. It felt wonderfully good. So good he could feel himself filling again, ready for another round. She moved against him, her body soft and pliable and scented with sex and sensuality.

He lifted his head and looked down at her. 'Hold that thought while I change the condom,' he said.

She gave him a shy smile. 'You're not too tired?'

'Not with you, sweetheart,' he said, deftly dealing with the condom exchange.

This time there was time to string out the pleasure of each caress. Marc explored her body all over again, taking her on a journey with him that was as exciting and as fulfilling as the last. When it was finally over he gathered her close in his arms and rested his chin on the top of her head as she drifted off to sleep. Sleep was not far off for him but there were still things he had on his mind…

Gemma woke up and stretched, and encountered a hair-roughened leg entwined with hers. Her heart gave a flying leap as she remembered what had happened earlier. She turned her head on the pillow and saw the sleeping form of Marc Di Angelo lying beside her. In sleep the hard angles and planes of his features softened, if anything making him look even more handsome. His mouth—her belly gave a little quiver when she recalled just where his mouth had been and how it had made her feel—was relaxed now as he breathed in and out evenly, his lips just slightly apart. He was in need of a shave. She had felt that when he had kissed her earlier. Her skin had reacted to the rough bristles, making her feel delightfully feminine. He had a tiny chickenpox scar just beneath his hairline and she placed her fingertip on it in a feather-light caress.

He opened one dark eye. 'Ready to play again?'

'You were playing possum!'

He rolled her over in one swift heart-stopping movement, his weight coming over her. 'I'm a light sleeper,' he said, dropping a hard, brief kiss to her mouth.

'Aren't you hungry?' Gemma asked.

'Starving,' he said, nibbling at her neck.

She shivered and gave herself up to his kiss. Food was suddenly the last thing on her mind.

But it must have been on his for after a few breathless moments he raised his mouth from hers. 'Let's eat and come back to bed and finish this.'

Gemma wrapped herself in a bathrobe, trying to disguise how shy she felt in front of him. It was one thing to sleep with a man but quite another to wander around without any clothes on. Thank God she'd shaved her legs.

Marc caught her by the tie of her bathrobe and tugged her back towards him where he was sitting on the bed, still naked. 'Hey,' he said, patting the bed beside him to indicate for her to sit down.

Gemma sat on the edge of the bed, clutching at the neck of the bathrobe to keep the edges together. 'Y-yes?'

He trailed a lazy finger down the curve of her terry-towelling-covered breast. 'You're beautiful. Every inch of you is beautiful.'

'Is that a line?'

'It's the truth.'

She looked into his darker-than-dark eyes. 'Thank you…'

He cupped her face and leaned in to kiss her again, a lingering kiss that set spot fires of wanting all through her being. 'You even taste beautiful,' he said, 'totally unforgettable, in fact.'

'So when you've gone back to Brisbane after your locum is done here, you might think of me now and again?' Gemma had intended it to sound light and flirty but instead it came out sounding petulant and needy.

He held her look for a heartbeat before he dropped his hands from her face and got off the bed and reached for his jeans.

'I'm sorry,' she said, chewing at her lips. 'I didn't mean that to sound quite the way it sounded.'

He zipped up his jeans with an action that had the dual effect of closing his fly as well as the conversation. 'I'll meet you downstairs,' he said. 'I have a couple of emails to check.'

Gemma sighed and flopped backwards on the bed, staring blindly at the ceiling. It seemed like she had a very long way to go before she had slick city sophistication down pat.

CHAPTER TEN

WHEN Gemma came downstairs Marc was dressed in his uniform and ready to leave for work. She wondered if he was rostered on or going out to avoid her. It was hard to tell what he was thinking. He had disclosed the tragic circumstances that had led him to take the post out here, but she still got the feeling he wasn't ready to have anyone get close to him other than physically.

'Gemma, we need to talk.'

She felt a wave of unease pass through her. 'It's all right, Marc,' she said. 'I understand the terms of our relationship. No one is holding a shotgun to your head.'

He came over to her and ran the back of his hand down her cheek, a soft caress that barely touched her but set every nerve alight. 'You deserve someone who can give you what you want,' he said. 'This is all I can give you. It's all I can give anyone.'

'I'm OK with that,' she said, even though she wasn't.

He looked at her for a long moment. 'If I had met you before…' He screwed his mouth up and his shoulders went down as he sighed.

'Before Simon's death?' Gemma asked.

He drew in a tight breath. 'I can't do that to you, Gemma. I can't destroy your life like Julie's was destroyed.'

'You're assuming something bad will happen,' Gemma said. 'That's a very cynical take on life, Marc. Not every cop gets killed on the job.'

His pain-filled eyes held hers for another long moment. 'When Julie opened the door that day she knew what I was going to say,' he said. 'She looked at me in that way that all victims of tragedy do. Her face sort of… collapsed. I see her face when I try and sleep at night. Not that I sleep, not properly. I lie there thinking of how I wish I could turn back the clock. It haunts me. I should have gone first. I should have known it was a serious domestic situation. I used to pride myself on picking them. I got it wrong. I got it so horribly wrong.'

'People aren't always predictable,' Gemma said. 'You had no way of knowing what was going to happen that day.'

'I see Sam's face too,' he went on, as if he wasn't listening to what Gemma was saying but was running a tape in his head that had been run time and time again. 'How am I going to tell him when he's older that I was the one who sent his father to his death? How can I go off and have a normal life when Julie's and Sam's lives have been destroyed?'

'Marc, you have to stop blaming yourself,' Gemma said. 'It's not helping you and it's not helping Julie and Sam. I don't think they would want you to be so unhappy and unfulfilled just because fate struck them a foul blow.'

'I was their best man,' he said, still on a roll. 'I can't bear the thought of getting married without Simon being there, as I was for him. I can't bear the thought of Julie and Sam standing in the pews, looking at the space where Simon should have been. I can't do it. I just can't do it.'

Gemma blinked back tears. 'You're being too hard on yourself, Marc.'

He breathed out another long deep sigh as he looked down at her. 'I guess I'll see you tonight.' He leaned down and pressed a kiss to her mouth, his dry lips clinging to hers as if they were not quite ready to let go.

Gemma touched her fingertips to her lips as she watched him drive away, her heart feeling as if it was being pressed together by two very large hands.

Narelle was one of the first to arrive to help with the clean-up. She had left Ben and Ruby with her mother so she could chip in, with Ray's help once he had finished his early shift. 'It was a fun night last night,' she said as she pulled down some streamers. 'Everyone seemed to have a good time, even your Marc.'

Gemma bundled up the paper tablecloth off the trestle. 'Mmm...'

Narelle came over and touched her on the arm. 'Hey, what's up? You seem preoccupied.'

'It's nothing,' Gemma said, forcing a smile. 'I'm just tired. It was a late night.'

Narelle wasn't fooled. 'OK, spill. What's going on with you and Marc?'

'Nothing... Well, nothing serious on his part.'

'But you're in love with him, right?' Narelle asked.

Gemma let out a deep sigh. 'If it's obvious to you, it must be obvious to everyone. I can't bear the thought of everyone feeling sorry for me when he finally leaves.'

'Maybe he'll stay or maybe you'll go with him,'

Narelle said. 'No one would blame you for heading off to the city for love.'

Gemma gave her a despondent look. 'He won't ask me to go with him. He travels alone. No ties. No commitments. It's how he lives his life. He's got baggage.'

'He's a cop,' Narelle said with a roll of her eyes. 'They've all got baggage.'

'This is big stuff,' Gemma said. 'He's punishing himself for what happened to his partner. His partner was killed on a job. Marc blames himself.'

Narelle frowned. 'He told you that?'

'Yes, last night,' Gemma said. 'He's determined to deny himself a normal life to make up for Simon, his partner, losing his. I tried to talk to him about it but he's made up his mind. I can tell. It's as if he wants to suffer. I can't seem to help him to see how pointless it is to punish himself. It's not helping him move on. It's not helping anyone.'

'I guess you just have to go with it,' Narelle said. 'He's opened up to you, which is always a good sign. Maybe he just needs some time. Stop worrying about what you might not get and enjoy what you have while you still have it.'

'But how long will I have it?' Gemma asked. 'I can't help feeling he might pull the plug on our relationship at any time.'

'You don't know that,' Narelle said. 'You're projecting your insecurities because of what happened with Stuart. Enjoy what you have with Marc. Everyone can see how perfectly suited you are. Just go with the flow for now. That's all you can do.'

'You're right,' Gemma said on a sigh. 'I need to go with it. I need to enjoy the journey instead of worrying about the destination.'

'Attagirl,' Narelle said, grinning. 'Now, where do you want me to put these streamers?'

Gemma was doing the washing-up later that evening when Marc came in. 'Hi,' she said, keeping her tone light and carefree. 'I've kept some dinner for you.'

'Thanks.'

She smiled and made to move past him but he caught her by the arm and turned her to face him. 'I've missed you,' he said, sliding his hand down her arm to capture her wrist. He brought it up to his mouth and kissed the sensitive underside, his eyes holding hers in a mesmerising lockdown.

'That's nice to know,' she said softly.

His tongue traced a slow circle against her pulse, making her shiver. He lowered her arm and pulled her close against him. The muscled wall of his chest brushed against her breasts, and his strong thighs pressed against hers, making hers tremble in reaction. His head came down and her eyelashes fluttered and then closed as his mouth sealed hers.

It was a hungry kiss with a drugging intensity. It swept Gemma away on its turbulent tide, stirring her senses into a frenzied response that left her breathless and aching with want. His tongue slipped through her lips, taking control of the kiss with commanding expertise, leaving no part of her mouth unexplored or unconquered. She kissed him back with fevered urgency, need racing along her veins at breakneck speed. Her inner core pulsed with desire, a low, deep throb that silently begged for assuagement.

'I want you so badly,' Marc said as he dragged his mouth off hers. 'I thought of nothing else the whole time I was at work.'

'Me too,' Gemma said.

The journey up the stairs was peppered with breathless interludes until Gemma was almost jumping out of her skin by the time he laid her on his bed.

He came down beside her, covering his mouth with hers as his hands worked their way under her shirt to cup her breasts. 'Mmm,' he said as he lifted his head a fraction. 'You feel so nice, so soft and warm and feminine.'

Gemma undid the buttons on his shirt, trailing her fingers down his chest to rediscover him. He was powerfully aroused by the time she got to his pelvis. He groaned as her fingers danced over him, moulding him and stroking him until he had to pull her hand away.

'You're wearing too many clothes,' he said, and proceeded to get rid of them for her.

As each item was removed she gave another gasp of pleasure as his mouth burned like fire against her exposed skin. Her breasts were subjected to a hot, moist, sensual assault that left her flesh singing. Her belly quivered as he moved his hand down to press against her, cupping her gently before he stroked her apart to slide one broad finger into the moist tight cave of her body. Her spine loosened at the caress and she gave another little whimper of delight as he tantalised her on her most sensitive point. Little ripples started out from deep inside her, radiating out until there was no part of her that wasn't carried away on the racing wave of release. She arched her spine, trying to prolong the exquisite moment, but eventually it faded, leaving her boneless.

'You're the most responsive lover I've ever had,' Marc said as he kissed his way back up her body.

'I guess I must be making up for lost time,' Gemma said, trying to keep things light and playful.

He looked down at her for a moment with an inscrutable expression on his face. 'Or is it that you're making the most of it while it lasts?'

The smile she pasted on her face felt tight and unnatural. 'Could be.'

He brushed an imaginary strand of hair off her face. 'Gemma…'

Gemma pushed a finger against his lips. 'Let's not talk about what can never be. Let's just enjoy what's here for now.'

He captured her finger with his lips, drawing it into his mouth in an erotic motion, his eyes holding hers in a moment of passionate intensity. He released her finger and brought his mouth back down to hers, kissing her until she was restless again, needing him to take her to the heights of pleasure all over again.

He rummaged for a condom and she helped this time to put it on, stroking and caressing him as she went, delighting in the way he responded with such potency. He might think she was incredibly responsive but Gemma felt sure he was equally so. He was breathing hard and fast with each movement of her hands, his eyes glittering with need as he drove hard into her body.

She held him to her, each erotic stroke of his body

within hers building her tension to a level she had not realised was possible. Every nerve in her body became taut, strung like wire stretched to snapping point. He pushed her over the edge with a deep groan against her neck, his body shuddering as hers quaked in the cataclysmic moments of heavenly, blissful, sexual pleasure.

Gemma listened to the sound of his heavy breathing, her arms still wrapped around him, holding her to him, wishing she never had to let him go. How soon would it be before he left town? Would she ever see him again? Would he look back at this time as just another notch on his bedpost or would he think of her as someone special, someone to be remembered as a perfect match physically? For that was what it felt like to her. He had shown her such passion, changing for ever how she would view intimacy. How could she ever find this with anyone else?

He rolled off her but brought her with him so she was lying over him. 'Hey.'

'Hey.'

He glanced at her mouth before going back to her eyes. 'Stay with me all night, Gemma,' he said. 'I'm not quite finished with you yet.'

Gemma gave him a coquettish look from beneath her lashes. 'Aren't we going to sleep?'

He swiftly turned her onto her back and covered her body with his. 'Eventually,' he said, and lowered his mouth to hers.

Gemma spent the next few days fielding comments from the locals on her relationship with the handsome sergeant. It was clear everyone was hoping Marc would stay and make an honest woman out of her. She laughed off their comments, trying desperately to keep things as casual as possible, even though daily she felt her love for him growing. It was the little things he did that made her realise what a special person he was and how much she was going to miss him when he moved on. She would come home after a long day of seeing patients to find he had cooked dinner, or he had bathed Flossie and picked all the grass seeds out of her coat. Another time he took Gemma on a picnic down to the swimming hole. It was one of the most romantic dates she had ever been on. He had brought wine and glasses and prepared the food himself. They swam together naked and then he made love to her while the sun sank in the west.

He never spoke of the future. He never spoke of his feelings. And although he was a sensitive and considerate lover, Gemma always felt he kept a part of himself separate. He was involved physically, but on an emotional level he wasn't touched, or certainly not as much as she was.

After another couple of weeks the investigation into the cliff accident took an interesting turn when Kate woke up from her coma. She was able to tell the police how her husband had asked her to pose for a photo close to the edge. She had been nervous about it as she didn't like heights. As to whether or not she had lost her footing or been pushed she was unable to say as her memory was affected from the cerebral swelling. She was determined to stick by her husband, however. She was furious about him being investigated and refused to assist the police any more with their enquiries.

'What do you think happened?' Gemma asked Marc when he had filled her in over dinner.

'It's hard to say,' he said. 'A lot of wives cover up for their husbands in difficult relationships. It wouldn't be the first time it's happened. She might genuinely believe he wasn't capable of it or she just can't remember.'

'Does it frustrate you that there's no clear-cut answer?' Gemma asked.

He toyed with the stem of his glass. 'A bit, but that's the job. Sometimes things don't work out the way you want them to.'

A little silence ticked past.

Marc looked across the table at her. 'Gemma, there's something I need to say to you.'

Gemma swallowed a tight restriction in her throat. 'Yes?'

His eyes looked shadowed and there was a frown pulling at his brow. 'I'm going back to Brisbane at the end of next week. I know it seems a bit sudden but I've been offered a new position. I've decided to take it.'

'You're leaving?' she asked, her heart thudding sickeningly. 'Just like that?'

He gave her a frustrated look. 'I've always been clear about my intention to return to the city,' he said. 'You can't say I didn't warn you.'

'But you've only been here just over a month,' she said.

'I've been here long enough to know this is not for me,' he said. 'It was always an interim appointment. Nothing has changed that.'

She gave him an embittered look. 'What you really

mean is you've been here long enough to know I am not for you. Isn't that more accurate?'

The line of his mouth became tense. 'Don't take it personally, Gemma. It's been fun but I have to get back to my life.'

'Your life?' She threw the words at him in scorn. 'What life is that? The one with the one-night stands and the one-too-many drinks and where you work ridiculous hours to somehow try and relieve your survivor guilt?'

His eyes narrowed to dark slits. 'You don't know what you're talking about.'

Gemma banged her hand on the table. 'Damn it, Marc, I do know what I'm talking about. You think I don't have regrets? You think I don't feel guilty about some of the patients I've lost or couldn't get to in time? It's life. It sucks. It sucks big time. We work in jobs that ask a lot of us, and we give it. We give it because it's not a career, it's a calling.'

He got up from the table, tossing down his napkin as if it was something distasteful. 'I didn't want things to end this way between us, Gemma,' he said.

She glared at him with eyes burning with banked-up tears. 'How were you going to end it, Marc?' she asked. 'By leaving a note on my pillow one morning? Or maybe a simple text message when you were safely at a distance? Is that more your style?'

He raked his fingers through his hair, leaving deep grooves. 'Don't make this any harder than it already is,' he said.

Gemma forced the words out through stiff lips. 'Is there someone else?'

His frown deepened. 'No, of course there isn't. This is about me, Gemma. It's not your fault. I want you to know that.'

'You have to forgive yourself, Marc,' Gemma said. 'You have to forgive yourself for not being the one that died that day.'

'Thanks for the tip,' he said coldly. 'I'll keep it in mind.'

She tightened her mouth. 'Maybe you should think about staying the rest of the time at the pub.'

'I've already spoken to Ron about it,' he said.

Gemma felt as if she had been punched in the stomach. 'Then don't let me keep you,' she said.

His eyes held hers for a tense moment. 'If ever you're in Brisbane—'

'I don't think so, Marc,' she said with a plastic smile. 'I think it's better if we make this a clean break.'

'As you wish.'

Gemma waited until he left before she allowed herself to cry. She felt foolish for being so hurt when all along she had known something like this would happen. But she loved him. She had hoped and hoped he would love her back. It didn't seem fair that he could walk away with such ease. He had walked out of her life without a backward glance. It was what he did best: walk away before he got too involved. It tore her heart out to think she would never see him again. He was letting his guilt ruin his life and hers too. She had never felt more helpless in her life. She couldn't reach him. For all the love she had for him she still hadn't been able to soothe the deep ache of his soul. Could anyone?

Flossie came over with a subdued look on her old face and Gemma dropped to her knees and wrapped her arms around the old dog's neck. 'Why does loving someone have to hurt so much?' she asked.

'Don't look at me like that,' Gemma said when she walked into the clinic. 'I'm sick of everyone looking at me as if I'm about to fall apart.'

'Oh, Gemma,' Narelle said. 'It's just that everyone is so worried about you. It's been three weeks since Marc left and you're still crying yourself to sleep at night.'

Gemma thrust her bag into the drawer under the desk. 'I do not cry myself to sleep at night.'

'You've got red eyes.'

'It's an allergy to dust.'

'Since when have you had a dust allergy?'

Gemma swung away to her consulting room. 'I don't want to be disturbed unless it's urgent. I haven't got anyone booked in until ten. I have some paperwork to sort out.'

'Hey, did you hear about Kate Barnes?' Narelle called out.

Gemma stopped and turned around. 'No. What's been going on?'

'She's accusing her husband of attempted murder.'

Gemma's eyes went wide. 'But I thought—'

'Marc was right,' Narelle said gravely. 'Jason Barnes waited for over two hours before he called for help. He thought Kate was dead. His plan was to kill her and collect the insurance. If it hadn't been for Marc's suspicion, Jason Barnes would have got away with it.'

'Did Kate remember more about that day or did the husband confess?'

'Kate overheard him talking to a friend about how his attempt on her life had failed but he was going to try again once the police backed off,' Narelle said.

Gemma bit her lip. 'That's awful… That poor girl…'

'Yeah, but how cool that Marc was on the money from the start,' Narelle said. 'We could do with more cops like him out in the bush. Surely the city could spare one or two now and again.'

Gemma gave an evasive nod and turned back to her consulting room. 'Nothing unless it's absolutely urgent, OK?'

Narelle swung the chair around and plonked her bottom down. 'Got it.'

Gemma had only worked through one pile of notes and could already hear the waiting room filling with patients when Narelle popped her head around the door. 'Sorry to disturb you but the waiting room is full, and you also have a visitor,' she said.

Gemma gave her a narrowed-eyed look. 'Is it an emergency?'

'Looks like it,' Narelle said. 'Will I send them in?'

'Can't be all that serious if they can walk to my office,' Gemma grumbled as she hauled herself to her feet.

The door opened and a tall figure stepped into the room. Gemma's heart did a stop start and her stomach dropped like an elevator. Her palms felt moist and yet her mouth was completely dry, so dry she couldn't speak.

'Hello, Gemma,' Marc said.

She swallowed to clear her blocked throat. 'Marc…'

His dark eyes ran over her. 'You've lost weight.'

'Yeah, cool, isn't it?' she said dryly. 'I've been trying to shift half a stone for three years. Just shows what a bit of discipline will do.'

His lips moved in a semblance of a smile. 'How's Flossie?'

'She's fine.'

'And you?'

She set her mouth. 'Can we get past this bit and go straight to why you're here?' she asked.

'I know you're still angry at me and I don't blame you, but if you'll just hear me out I'll try and—'

'I'm not angry at you,' she said. 'I'm angry at myself. You told me the terms and I still went ahead and fell in love with you. I know it was my fault. You never made any promises. I'm the stupid romantic, remember? I was the one who was caught up in the romantic fantasy of falling for the handsome stranger who strode into town. Congratulations on the case, by the way. Narelle told me you finally got your guy.'

'Thank you, but I would much rather get my girl.'

She looked at him with her mouth open, unable to speak for a moment or two. 'Wh-what did you say?'

His dark eyes softened as they held hers. 'I was worried you would hate me by now,' he said. 'God knows, I deserve it, walking out on you like that.'

'I don't hate you, Marc,' she said. 'I wish I could. Maybe I wouldn't be the object of everyone's pity if I stomped around town telling everyone how much I hate you.'

'I got the impression I wasn't exactly welcome around here any more,' Marc said. 'Ron just gave me a serve and so did Maggie Innes. She told me in no uncertain terms that if I didn't do the right thing by you, she would run me out of town herself.'

'It's been a very long time since Maggie was able to run anywhere,' Gemma said with a wry smile.

His eyes softened even more. 'I've missed that.'

She frowned. 'What?'

Marc stepped up close and traced a fingertip over her lips. 'Your smile,' he said. 'It's like sunshine. It lightens up the dark corners of my soul.'

Gemma had tried to keep her hopes in check but they kept filling up the space inside her chest until she could barely breathe. 'Why are you here, Marc?' she asked.

He took both of her hands in his. 'Because I wanted to see you again,' he said. 'I wanted to tell you how much I love you.'

Gemma just stared at him, her mouth falling open again.

He squeezed her hands and continued, 'I went back to Brisbane determined to throw myself at my new job but a week in I knew I had made a mistake. I toughed it out for another week, and then I went and saw Simon's wife Julie. I'd been avoiding her and Sam for months. I know she was hurt by it but I just couldn't bear being around them in their grief. It made mine so much more unbearable, the guilt too.'

'What did she say?' Gemma asked.

'Much the same as you said—I was punishing myself and it wouldn't bring Simon back. It was taking away two lives instead of one. She told me Simon had always told her he was prepared for the worst. He wanted her to get on with her life if the worst happened. She's taking baby steps to do that. She told me I wasn't helping anyone by blaming myself for something that so easily could have gone the other way.'

'Sensible girl.'

He smiled at her. 'Yes, she is, and she's looking forward to meeting you at the wedding.'

Gemma frowned again. 'Wedding? What wedding?'

He brought her hands up to his chest and held them against his thudding heart. 'Our wedding, sweetheart,' he said. 'You'll marry me, won't you? I've travelled all this way to ask you in person. You can't possibly say no to me.'

Gemma pursed her lips in a mock muse. 'Hmm… Not sure about the proposal,' she said. 'I think maybe I need a second opinion.'

'Where are we going?' Marc asked as she dragged him by the hand out of her consulting room to the waiting room, where it seemed half of Jingilly Creek was gathered.

'Ask me again,' Gemma said. 'I need witnesses. I need to know I wasn't just imagining it.'

Marc looked at the sea of faces, the previously buzzing waiting room suddenly silent, and then back at the woman he loved with every cell of his being. 'Gemma Kendall, will you marry me and live as my wife in Jingilly Creek, serving this community for as long as we both shall live?' he asked.

Gemma's smile lit up the room as well as Marc's

heart. 'Sergeant Marc Di Angelo,' she said as she stepped up on tip-toe to reach his mouth, 'I thought you'd never ask.'

EPILOGUE

IT WAS a beautiful day for late winter, bright and sunny with fluffy white clouds drifting over the cerulean blue sky. The shearing shed was decked out with flowers flown in from the city—roses and jasmine, their fragrance heavy and spicy in the air.

Marc waited at the makeshift altar, his eyes going to Julie, who was standing with little Sam's hand in hers, her face beaming. He winked at Sam, who grinned back, and then he turned to look at his family. His mother was crying but that was what she always did at weddings, christenings, birthdays and even a barbeque on one occasion. His father smiled an I'm-proud-of-you-son smile that made Marc's heart swell. His sisters were craning their necks to catch the first glimpse of Gemma. They weren't at all interested in him now they were soon to have a much-adored sister-in-law to fuss over. They adored her as much as she adored them. His nephews and nieces too had taken to her like she was the best thing that had ever happened since toys were invented.

And then his bride stepped into view. His breath caught in his throat as he saw Gemma walk towards him, step by step, her beautiful face shining with love for him. It had been her idea to get married in the shearing shed. And it was her idea not to have attendants but for them to come together in marriage alone. It was another one of the things he loved most about her. She was so sensitive and understanding, always letting him have the time he needed to heal and move on. He wasn't totally there yet but he was close. So very close.

The pastor had travelled all the way from Minnigarra to conduct the service and it was as meaningful and sacred as any city cathedral could have offered. The solemn vows were exchanged in voices that wobbled and cracked in places but somehow that just made it all the more special. Marc knew firsthand what 'till death do us part' meant. But, then, so did Gemma. At times her job was dangerous and that was something he'd had to come to terms with. They were on a journey together and no one could predict the future, but that wasn't what was important. The here and now was important: the journey, not the destination.

'You may kiss the bride.'

The words drew a collective indulgent sigh from the congregation as Marc brought his mouth down to Gemma's, sealing their commitment with a kiss that was full of love and hope for the future.

Gemma looked up at him once the kiss was over, her eyes glistening with happy tears. 'Is this a good time to tell you I love you?' she asked.

He smiled down at her. 'It's a great time,' he said, not in the least surprised or embarrassed that his voice broke over the words. Emotion was something else Gemma had patiently waited for him to embrace. He said it all the time now and it felt so good. 'I love you too.'

She gave him a sheepish look from beneath her lashes. 'I have to tell you something else but maybe now is not the right time…'

Marc felt a flutter of excitement inside. 'Sweetheart, you can tell me anything any time, you know that.'

She smiled with joy as she looked into his eyes. 'I'm having a baby,' she said. She did a little happy dance in front of him. 'Can you believe it?'

Marc felt his eyes go moist. 'Are you sure?'

Her eyes were bright with happiness. 'I did the test this morning.'

He squeezed her hands, holding them close to his heart. 'Is this a good time to tell our guests?' he said with a proud smile.

Gemma's eyes twinkled as she and Marc turned to face their friends and family. Marc opened his mouth to speak but before he could get out a word the congregation erupted in rapturous deafening applause.

Marc looked down at his beautiful bride, his eyes crinkled in amusement. 'I guess they must have already known.'

Gemma smiled. 'Some things are just plain obvious, don't you think?'